DISNEY · PIXAR
STORYBOOK
COLLECTION

DISNEY PRESS

New York

Table of Contents

WALL·E

Blast Into Adventure

On Earth, a robot named WALL-E gathered trash. It was the twenty-ninth century and the humans had left behind a lot of trash. Now they were up in space aboard a giant space liner called the Axiom.

Robots like WALL-E had been left on Earth to clean up the mess. But now WALL-E was the only bot left.

Suddenly a spaceship touched down, and a sleek white robot named EVE got off. She had been sent from the Axiom to see if enough trash had been cleared so that humans could live on Earth again.

WALL-E was curious about EVE. She was very serious.

WALL-E showed her all the things he had found while cleaning up the trash, such as a lightbulb and a broken clock. He even danced with a garbage-can lid and made her giggle.

Then WALL-E showed her a plant he had found. EVE took it and shut down at once. WALL-E did his best to care for his new friend. But it was no use. She wouldn't respond. When the spaceship returned for EVE, WALL-E hid and went into space with her.

Aboard the Axiom, the plant had somehow disappeared. The Captain ordered EVE to go to the repair ward.

He spotted WALL-E and sent him to be cleaned.

WALL-E watched as the robots started to repair EVE. It looked as if they were hurting her. WALL-E crashed into the repair room and rescued her and the other robots in the repair ward who were called reject-bots. They were all grateful to WALL-E.

But nobody else on the Axiom was happy. They wanted to punish WALL-E and EVE. The steward-bots caught up with them, but the reject-bots helped their two friends get away.

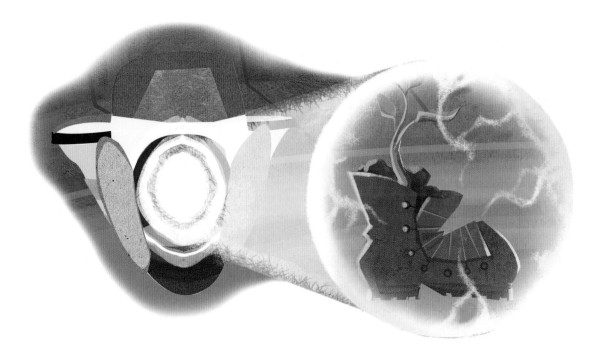

EVE decided that the safest place for WALL-E was back on Earth, so she led him to an escape pod. But WALL-E didn't want to leave EVE behind.

As EVE tried to convince WALL-E to get inside, they heard someone coming and hid. It was Gopher, the Captain's assistant-bot. He had the missing plant! He put it in the escape pod and set the pod to launch and then self-destruct. He didn't want the plant to live.

Gopher exited the pod to press the LAUNCH button. WALL-E hurried aboard to try to get the plant back. But he wasn't fast enough. The pod launched with WALL-E inside!

"Pod will self-destruct in ten seconds," a computer voice said. WALL-E pressed all kinds of buttons, trying to escape.

At the same time, EVE was rocketing toward the pod, hoping to catch up to WALL-E. But she was still far behind when—*KA-BOOM!*—the pod exploded.

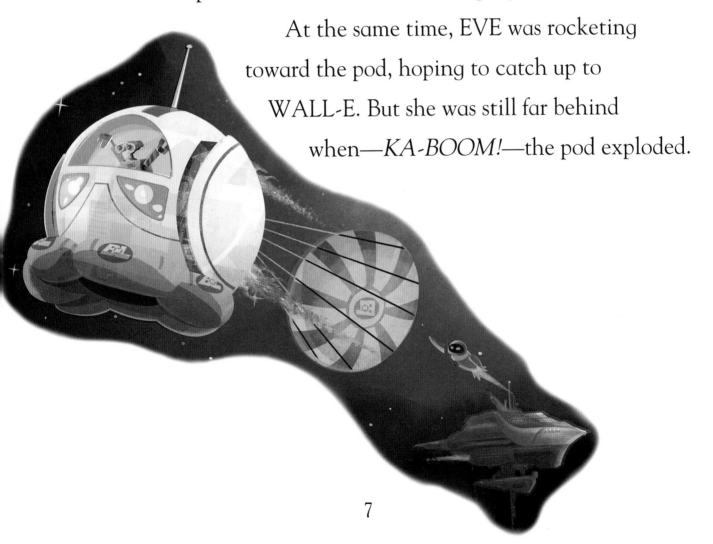

7

A moment later, WALL-E blasted toward EVE using a fire extinguisher from the escape pod. EVE was pleased to see WALL-E and the plant safe and sound. She leaned toward him and a spark passed between their heads. WALL-E was thrilled as the two danced dreamily in space.

Back on the Axiom, EVE told WALL-E to stay hidden while she brought the plant to the Captain. The Captain was excited: if a plant could grow on Earth, then it was time for people to return!

The Captain gave the order to turn on the ship's holo-detector. It would identify the plant.

If the plant was from Earth, the Axiom would go there. Auto, the autopilot, refused. He was following orders from the head of Buy-n-Large, BnL, the superstore back on Earth that had built the Axiom centuries earlier. The people at BnL had told everyone they would clean up all of the trash on Earth.

But BnL had broken their promise. The work had proved to be too much. They had abandoned Earth and sent secret orders to the Axiom autopilot never to return to the planet.

It had been Auto who had made the plant "disappear" earlier. He had told Gopher to launch it into space so that the Captain wouldn't ask any more questions! Now Gopher tossed the plant down a garbage chute. But WALL-E, who had been climbing up the chute to find EVE, saved the plant once again.

When Auto saw what had happened, he zapped WALL-E, and turned off EVE. They both went down the garbage chute.

After sitting in his hover chair for years and having robots do everything for him, the Captain was too weak to stop Auto. The robot had complete control of the ship.

Down in the garbage bay, WALL-E was in bad shape. He needed some spare parts. EVE knew where to find them: back on Earth in his trailer. WALL-E had helped her. Now it was her turn to help him. Using her blaster arm to fire, she made a hole in the ceiling. She had to get the plant to the holo-detector and bring the Axiom back to Earth.

WALL-E and EVE dodged the stewards with more help
from the reject-bots, while the Captain struggled with Auto for
control of the bridge. "EVE, WALL-E," the Captain said in a
shipwide announcement, "bring the plant to the lido deck. I'll
have activated the holo-detector."

Sure enough, when WALL-E and EVE got there, the holo-detector was activated! But then Auto overpowered the Captain again, and the holo-detector began to sink back into the floor. A very weak WALL-E jammed himself under the holo-detector to hold it up.

Meanwhile, on the bridge, the Captain was gathering all his strength. He couldn't remember ever getting out of his hover chair. But he had to try. Like a baby taking his first steps, he stood up, walked over to Auto, and turned him off!

The Axiom passengers saw it all on their holo-screens and cheered!

EVE got the plant into the holo-detector. "Plant origin verified," said a computer voice. "Course set for Earth."

The Axiom hyperjumped back to Earth in no time flat. But EVE didn't know if she could save WALL-E. She flew him to his trailer and replaced his damaged parts. Then she blasted a hole in the trailer roof, recharging his battery with sunlight. WALL-E powered up!

But he didn't seem himself. He didn't recognize EVE, or he didn't care. All he cared about was trash: scooping trash, compacting trash, stacking trash. It was as if he had forgotten about his adventures with EVE.

EVE called his name, grasped his hand, and tried to snap him out of it. But nothing worked. As if saying a last good-bye, EVE leaned toward him. A spark passed between their heads as it had once before. Then EVE turned to go.

But WALL-E didn't let go. He was still holding EVE's hand. She turned to look at WALL-E and saw his eyes light up. His hand was clasped around hers. "Eee-vah?" he said.

"WALL-E!" EVE cried.

Meanwhile, near the ship, the Captain was planting the small plant that had led them all back to Earth. The Captain, the passengers of the Axiom, and all the robots had a lot of work ahead of them. It wouldn't be easy to finish the job of cleaning up the planet. But now, WALL-E wouldn't be doing it alone.

With EVE at his side, WALL-E knew he would never feel lonely again.

The Big Search

One day, a little clown fish named Nemo went on a field trip. His classmates dared each other to swim toward a boat that was anchored nearby. Nemo's father, Marlin, warned his son not to go, but Nemo didn't listen. He was tired of his dad thinking he was too little to do anything.

Marlin was overprotective of his son. Nemo had been the only survivor when a barracuda attacked Nemo's mother and a nestful of eggs she had laid. Plus, Nemo's right fin had always been smaller than the left one, which worried Marlin even more.

As Marlin called out to him, Nemo reached the boat and slapped it with his fin.

Just then, a scuba diver snatched Nemo. Before Marlin knew it, his son was gone. "Nemo!" he cried. "No! No!" Marlin swam after the boat, but it quickly disappeared.

"Help me!" Marlin shouted to a group of fish who were swimming by. "Has anybody seen a boat?"

Finally, a regal blue tang fish named Dory stopped to help. "It went this way," she said. "Follow me."

But Dory was a very forgetful fish. She led Marlin in circles because she couldn't remember anything. Marlin decided that following Dory wasn't going to help him find his son. He turned to go—and came face-to-face with a big shark!

The shark took Dory and Marlin to a sunken submarine to meet his two friends. Marlin was worried that the sharks would attack them. But the sharks said they were trying to learn not to eat other fish.

Then Marlin spotted the mask of the scuba diver. He remembered seeing one fall from the boat that had taken Nemo before it sped away. Dory wanted to see if the sharks could read the writing on it, but Marlin didn't. He still didn't trust the sharks. Dory and Marlin struggled over the mask so much that it hit Dory's nose and made it bleed a little.

Once the shark named Bruce smelled blood, he couldn't control himself. Now he wanted to eat Dory and Marlin! Bruce chased the two fish while his friends tried to stop him. Finally they managed to escape.

But their adventures weren't over yet. Dory and Marlin still had the mask with the writing on it. Luckily, Dory remembered that she knew how to read. Just then, she accidentally dropped the mask. The two fish swam after it into deep, dark water. Soon, they spotted a glowing ball. As they swam closer, they saw that the ball was attached to a scary anglerfish. Marlin tried to distract the anglerfish so Dory could read the writing on the mask. "Speed-read!" he commanded.

Dory read: "P. Sherman, 42 Wallaby Way, Sydney."

Sydney! That had to be where Nemo was. The anglerfish charged. Marlin and Dory held the mask up. The anglerfish slammed into it and ended up trapped with the mask on its face. Marlin and Dory quickly swam away.

Marlin decided he should go to Sydney alone. Dory was
always forgetting things, and she took a long time to do
everything. He needed to get to Nemo as soon as possible,
so he told Dory he would go on without her.

"You mean you don't like me?" Dory asked. She started to
cry. A group of moonfish overheard what Marlin had said and
swam over to comfort Dory. When Marlin asked them how to
get to Sydney, they wouldn't give him directions.

But when Dory asked, they
pointed in the direction of the
East Australian Current. Marlin
decided to let Dory go
with him, after all.

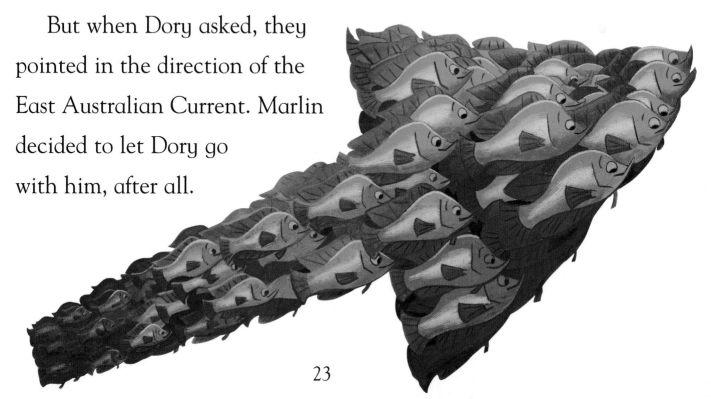

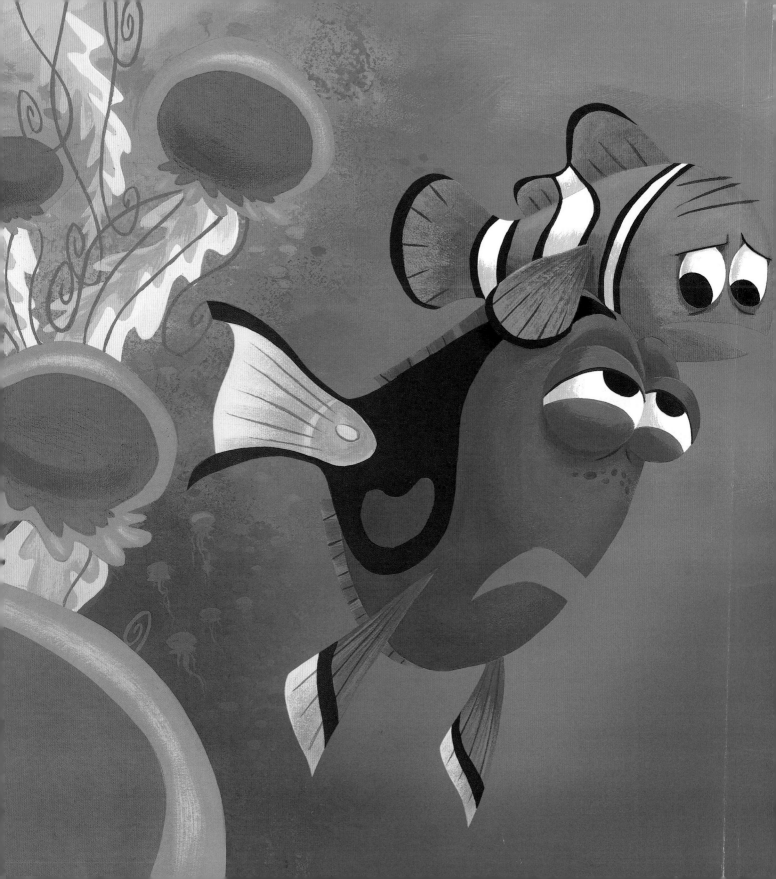

Marlin had already started swimming away when one of the moonfish gave Dory a tip. "When you come to a trench, swim *through* it, not *over* it," he warned.

Soon, Dory and Marlin came to the trench, and Marlin wanted to swim over it. Dory thought that was wrong, but she couldn't remember why, so they went with Marlin's plan.

As they swam over the trench, they were surrounded by a school of jellyfish. Marlin dodged their stinging tentacles, but when he turned around, he didn't see Dory. "Dory?" he called. He retraced his steps and found that she had been trapped by a jellyfish. Marlin was stung several times as he pulled his friend to safety.

Marlin and Dory were really tired from the jellyfish encounter. They drifted for a while, and soon everything went black.

When Marlin woke up, he was on the shell of a giant sea turtle named Crush. Dory was riding on the shell of another turtle. There were tons of turtles—all swimming the East Australian Current toward Sydney.

"Takin' on the jellies—awesome!" Crush exclaimed. Marlin told the younger turtles about how he was swimming the ocean to find his missing son.

The turtles told other turtles, and the news was passed from one sea creature to another.

Dory and Marlin rode on the turtles' shells for a while. Before they knew it, the turtles were dropping them off near Sydney.

As they swam through the murky water, they got lost. Dory decided to ask a whale for help. But as the whale approached, it quickly swallowed them.

Marlin was frantic. "I have to get out! I have to find my son!" he cried.

Then the whale began to groan. It swam to the surface, and water came out of its spout along with Marlin and Dory. They looked around. The whale had taken them to Sydney Harbor.

The two fish looked all night for the boat that had taken Nemo, but they couldn't find it. The next morning, they were scooped up by a pelican.

The pelican wanted to eat them, but Marlin had had enough. "I didn't come this far to be breakfast!" he cried. He and Dory struggled until the pelican finally let them go. "I gotta find my son, Nemo!" Marlin yelled.

Another pelican, named Nigel, overheard Marlin. "I know where your son is," he said. He had heard lots of stories about a dad who was braving his way through the ocean to find his son. Plus, he'd met Nemo himself, at a dentist's office, where the little clown fish was living in a fish tank.

Nigel put some water in his beak, picked up Marlin and Dory, and flew toward Wallaby Way. When they got to the office, they saw Nemo, but he looked like he was dead.

Marlin didn't know that Nemo had been pretending to be dead so that he could get back to the ocean. The dentist pushed Nigel out the window.

In the chaos, Nemo fell onto a tray. After a struggle with the dentist's bratty niece, Darla, and with some help from the other fish in the tank, Nemo was catapulted into the dentist's sink. He went down the drain. "Don't worry!" shouted one of the tank fish. "All drains lead to the ocean!"

Since Marlin thought Nemo was gone, he asked Nigel to drop him and Dory back in the harbor. Marlin was heartbroken. He thought he'd lost Nemo. He thanked Dory for her help and told her that it was time for them to go their separate ways. "I'm sorry," he said, "but I want to forget."

31

At that moment, Nemo popped out of a sewer drain in the harbor and into the claws of some crabs. Luckily he escaped and ran into Dory. She didn't know who Nemo was at first. Then she spotted a sign on a pipe that said "Sydney," and remembered everything. Nemo was the fish they'd been searching for!

She had to get Nemo and his father back together! Dory and Nemo swam quickly and caught up with Marlin.

"Nemo!" Marlin cried.

"Daddy!" Nemo shouted. They were so happy to see each other. Just then, Dory got caught in a fishing net, along with a school of grouper fish. Thinking quickly, Nemo swam into the net. Marlin was worried his son would get hurt, but Nemo convinced his dad he could help. As Nemo yelled "Swim down!" to the other fish, Marlin joined in.

The fish swam downward and the net broke. All the fish were free! Marlin swam to Nemo.

Marlin was overjoyed to have his Nemo back again. And
during the search, he'd made some amazing friends, especially
Dory—even if she couldn't always remember who he was!

Off the Fast Track

Beep! Beep! Lightning McQueen, the fastest race car around, awoke with a start. Cars were honking at him. Suddenly, he saw the headlights of a big truck. It was headed straight for him! Lightning panicked but managed to veer out of the way. He realized he had been driving the wrong way on the Interstate!

Earlier that day, Lightning had ended up in a three-way tie for first place in the biggest race of the year, the Dinoco 400. He got into his trailer and took off with his driver, Mack, for California right away. That was the site of the tiebreaker. Lightning was a rookie race car and this was his shot at  fame and fortune. He wanted to get there as quickly as possible.

So he made Mack drive all night instead of stopping to rest.

Along the way, Lightning had dozed off. Now here he was, careening down the wrong lane of the Interstate.

Lightning began to search for Mack. He saw a truck going down an exit ramp and followed it. But when he caught up, he realized it wasn't Mack, after all.

He drove back toward the Interstate. Then he heard sirens wailing behind him. *Woo-woo!* He slowed down, thinking Sheriff could point him in the right direction.

But when Sheriff's tailpipe backfired, Lightning thought he was being shot at!

Lightning zigged and zagged as fast as he could, trying to avoid the bullets he thought were headed toward him. The next thing the race car knew, he had driven into a sleepy-looking town.

"What?" he cried. "That's not the Interstate!" He realized he'd been going the wrong way. He raced into the quiet town with Sheriff still chasing him.

Suddenly, Lightning saw a line of traffic cones in front of him. He swerved to avoid them, which caused him to spin. Then he smashed into a fence, some tires, and a statue, and ended up dangling from two telephone poles. Along the way, he'd done all kinds of damage, including ruining the town's main road.

Sheriff rolled up to him. "Boy, you're in a heap of trouble," he said.

When Lightning woke up the next morning, he was locked in the local impound lot. He tried to move but couldn't. A yellow parking boot was on his tire!

Lightning looked up
and saw a rusty tow truck.
"Where am I?" he asked.

"You're in Radiator
Springs, the cutest
little town in Carburetor
County!" replied the tow truck, whose name was Mater.

Lightning looked around. The town looked old and run-down to
him. And this tow truck didn't seem very smart.

"You know," said Lightning, getting an idea, "I'd love to see the
rest of the town, so if you could just open the gate, take this boot off,
you and me—we'll go cruisin', check out the local scene."

"Cool!" cried Mater. He started to open the gate until a loud,
stern voice stopped him.

"Mater! Quit your yappin' and tow this delinquent road hazard
to traffic court." It was Sheriff.

Before long, Lightning was standing in front of Doc Hudson, the town's judge. Sheriff had told Lightning to expect to be put away for good.

"I want him out of our town!" Doc yelled, when he found out Lightning was a race car.

Just then, a sleek, blue sports car rolled in. Lightning thought she was from his lawyer's office. "Thanks for coming," he told her, "but we're all set. He's letting me go."

"Letting you go?" she asked in disbelief. It turned out she was Sally, the town's attorney, and she wanted the road fixed. She convinced everyone that the town's survival depended on it.

In the end, Doc told Lightning that he had to repair the damaged road before he could leave.

Lightning was not happy. When he saw Bessie, the massive, steaming, dripping, road-paving machine he'd have to pull, he decided to make a run for it.

As soon as Mater took off his parking boot, Lightning sped away. Unfortunately, he didn't get too far—his gas tank had been emptied.

With no other choice, Lightning got to work. Sheriff hitched him up to Bessie, then the race car inched along as hot tar oozed onto the road. Lightning hated it.

The race car pulled Bessie along as quickly as he could. Soon he had finished, but the road was all bumpy.

"The deal was, you fix the road," Doc said sternly, "not make it worse. Start over."

Lightning couldn't take it anymore. "Hey, look, Grandpa, I'm not a bulldozer. I'm a race car," he replied.

"Then why don't we just have a little race, me and you?" Doc challenged him. "If you win, you go, and I fix the road. If I win, you do the road my way."

This was it—Lightning's chance to get to California in time for the big race! All he had to do was beat this old clunker. "You know what, old-timer?" he replied confidently. "That's a wonderful idea. Let's race." Lightning, Doc, and all the cars from town drove to Willy's Butte.

"Speed. I am speed," Lightning repeated as he revved his engine. The flag dropped and the race car bolted.

When the dust cleared, Doc was still at the starting line. "Come on, Mater," Doc said. "Might need a little help."

Mater and Doc started after the race car, taking their time. Meanwhile, Lightning had zoomed ahead and was approaching the turn around the butte. But then, just as he started into the sharp left turn, he lost control and went soaring over a steep ledge—straight into a cactus grove.

A few minutes later, Doc and Mater peered down at the race car. "You drive like you fix roads!" Doc yelled down to him. "Lousy." Then, he drove away and left Mater to tow Lightning out.

Later that night, Lightning was angrily scraping the bumpy asphalt off the road. "You race like you fix roads," Lightning sputtered to himself, repeating Doc's words. "I'll show him. I *will* show him."

The next morning, the cars of Radiator Springs woke up to find a brand-new, perfectly smooth section of road. Even Doc was impressed. He looked over at Bessie, who was sitting quietly. Where was Lightning?

Just then, Doc heard the sound of a race car in the distance.

Doc headed over to the butte where Lightning had wiped out
the day before, and saw the race car practicing that sharp left
turn. Lightning was determined to find a way to make the turn.
But he just kept crashing.

Doc decided to give the young race car some
advice. "This is dirt," he told him. "You have to
turn right to go left."

Lightning thought this was bad advice, especially since it came from an old car who didn't know a thing about racing. But the next time he got to the turn, he tried Doc's suggestion at the very last minute—and sailed off the cliff into the cactuses. He hadn't done what Doc told him early enough to make it work.

Later, Lightning got back to work. But he noticed a change in the other cars. They were nicer now that he had started to fix the road. They'd started sprucing up their stores, too.

That night, Mater decided Lightning needed to have some fun. So they went to a field filled with sleeping tractors. Then Mater snuck up to one and honked his horn. *Beeeep!* The tractor woke up with a start, tipped over, and snorted. Mater laughed and laughed. Then he said it was Lightning's turn. The race car didn't have a horn, so he revved his engine loudly. *Vroom, vroom!* All the tractors tipped over at once. *Snort! Snort! Snort!*

On the way home, Mater showed the race car how to drive backward. Lightning couldn't remember the last time he'd had so much fun.

The next morning, Lightning peeked into Doc's garage and discovered that Doc had once been a Piston Cup champion. When Doc found Lightning there, he got angry and wouldn't talk about his racing days.

Later, Sally took Lightning for a drive. They stopped for a rest at an overlook, and Lightning noticed that the Interstate bypassed Radiator Springs. "They're driving right by," he said sadly. "They don't even know what they're missing."

Sally told him she dreamed of the town becoming prosperous again—the way it had been before the Interstate was built.

When they returned to town, Lightning realized what a great time he'd had. "Thanks for the drive," he said. "It's kind of nice to slow down every once in a while."

A little while later, Lightning caught Doc secretly racing at the butte. He looked amazing. Doc told the rookie how the racing world had forgotten about him after he'd had a big crash.

"Hey, look, Doc, I'm not one of them," Lightning said.

"When is the last time you cared about something except yourself, hot rod?" Doc demanded.

Lightning was speechless.

The next morning, the road was completely finished.

Sheriff offered to escort Lightning out of town so he could get to his big race on time, but Lightning wasn't ready to leave yet. First, he needed a new set of tires. Luigi, the tire shop owner, was thrilled! Lightning was the first customer he'd had in years.

After getting a new set of whitewalls, Lightning stopped at every store in town. He got gas at Fillmore's Organic Fuel, tried out some night-vision goggles at Sarge's Surplus Hut, and got a brand-new paint job at Ramone's body shop.

"*Ka-chow!*" Lightning said with a laugh. He was glad he'd gotten to help all of his new friends.

That night, Lightning and the rest of the town surprised Sally. They had fixed all the neon signs, and when she arrived, they turned them on. Sally watched delightedly as the cars cruised along Main Street. The town looked like it had in its heyday.

Lightning was happier than he'd ever been on a racetrack. The town had taught him that winning races and being the fastest car weren't as important as having good friends and enjoying life.

THE INCREDIBLES

The Supers
Save The Day

In the city of Municiburg, everyone slept soundly at night. That's because they knew that the Supers, a group of heroes with special powers, would keep them safe.

One night, Mr. Incredible, a Super who was incredibly strong, was on his way to his wedding when he heard about a robbery that was in progress. He tried to stop the thief. While he was there, a boy named Buddy flew in using some rocket boots that he'd made.

He didn't have any powers, but he was determined to become Mr. Incredible's sidekick.

But the Super didn't want a sidekick. "I work alone," he said. "Go home."

Buddy didn't listen. He tried to show how helpful he could be, and the bank robber got away. Mr. Incredible was upset and made it very clear he didn't want Buddy's help ever again.

Then Mr. Incredible went to the church. He was getting married to Elastigirl, a Super who could stretch her body into all kinds of shapes. He was very late, but she forgave him, and they married in front of their Super friends. They were very happy together.

One day, Mr. Incredible saved someone who didn't want to be saved. He was sued, and it wasn't long before the rest of the Supers were sued for their good deeds, too. The government decided the lawsuits were too expensive. So, they put all of the heroes in the Super Relocation Program and gave them new names and regular jobs. The only condition was that they couldn't use their powers. That way no one would ever find out who they really were—and no one could sue them.

Mr. Incredible and Elastigirl became Bob and Helen Parr. They lived in the suburbs and had a house and three kids— Violet, Dash, and Jack-Jack. They tried to live a normal life, but sometimes things got a little crazy around the house. After all, Violet could generate force fields and turn invisible, and Dash had Super speed. Little Jack-Jack didn't seem to have any powers yet.

Bob worked at an insurance company, but he missed his old life. One night, he and his friend Lucius, who'd been a Super called Frozone, used their powers to save some people from a fire. Unfortunately, they didn't realize someone was watching them from the shadows. . . .

Before long, the person who'd seen them contacted Bob. Her name was Mirage and she knew that he'd been a Super. She had a top secret job for him. Bob decided to take it. After all, he missed doing Super work.

Bob put on his old Super suit and told Helen he was going on a business trip. Then he got on a plane with Mirage and they flew to an island. She told him it was a government testing facility and they'd lost control of an experimental robot called the Omnidroid.

"It's a learning robot," she told him. "Every moment you spend fighting it only increases its knowledge of how to beat you."

Mr. Incredible used all of his strength against the Omnidroid. He was finally able to trick it into defeating itself.

When Mr. Incredible went home, he felt like a new man. He started to work out and got his old friend Edna Mode to design him a new-and-improved Super suit.

Soon, Bob got another call from Mirage about more work on the island, and he eagerly agreed to go. But when he got there, he realized he'd been set up. It turned out that Mirage's boss was

Buddy, the same boy who'd wanted to be Mr. Incredible's sidekick long ago. But he wasn't a boy any longer. He'd grown up, and now he called himself Syndrome. He was still bitter about how Mr. Incredible had treated him.

"All I wanted was to help you!" Syndrome cried. He'd invented the Omnidroid and had an evil plan to use it to become more powerful. He tried to capture Mr. Incredible, but the Super escaped. Later, he snuck back into Syndrome's headquarters to learn more about the villain's scheme. It wasn't long before Syndrome found him and trapped him with giant blobs of goo.

Meanwhile, back at home, Helen began to suspect that Bob was up to something. She went to visit Edna Mode, who explained that she'd just made Bob a new Super suit. In fact, she'd designed suits for the whole family!

"Each suit contains a homing device," the designer explained.

Helen left the children with a babysitter and activated the device. Then she put on her Super suit and borrowed a jet. As she flew toward the homing signal, she discovered that Dash and Violet had stowed away with her.

Just then, a missile hit the plane. Syndrome had seen them! The plane went down, and Elastigirl and the children landed in the ocean. Elastigirl turned herself into the shape of a boat, and Dash used his Super speed to power them through the water.

When they got to shore, Elastigirl left the children in a cave and told them to stay put. Then she went to find her husband.

While Helen was gone, Syndrome launched a rocket. Its exhaust traveled through the cave Violet and Dash were in. The children escaped just in time and ended up in a jungle. Soon, they set off one of Syndrome's alarms.

It wasn't long before guards came after them. "Dash, run!" Violet yelled. She turned herself invisible and hurried away.

Dash took off in a blur of motion. This was the first time he'd ever used his powers against bad guys. The guards went after him in flying ships called velocipods. Dash grabbed a vine and swung on it, but it snapped. "*Aaaaah!*" he screamed as he fell. He hit the top of a velocipod. He punched the guard, then jumped off the ship right before it hit a cliff. Then he zoomed across the top of the ocean and back to the jungle, where he ran into Violet.

She put a force field around them, and together they fought the guards as best they could.

Inside Syndrome's headquarters, Elastigirl had located her husband. Mirage had just released him from his prison cell. Mirage had finally realized just how evil Syndrome really was. She warned Mr. Incredible and his wife that their kids had set off the security alarms.

Mr. Incredible and Elastigirl raced to the jungle to save their children. When they got there, they saw that Violet and Dash were using their powers on the guards—and holding their own!

Mr. Incredible and Elastigirl joined in the fight. The family was winning—until Syndrome showed up. The villain used an immobi-ray on them so that they couldn't move. Then he trapped them in high-tech suspension beams and flew off to the city of Metroville—where the Omnidroid was already wreaking havoc.

Syndrome planned to prove to everyone that he was a hero by showing up and defeating the robot.

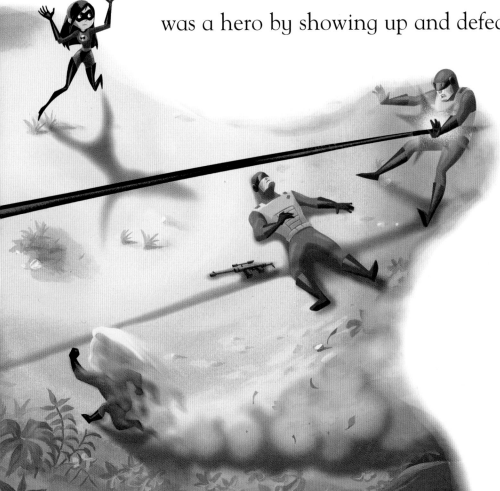

No one would ever know that he'd made the robot—and he'd become a bigger hero than Mr. Incredible ever had been.

Luckily, Violet was able to use a force field to break the immobi-ray's hold on her. She freed the rest of her family, and they flew to the city in a van that was attached to a rocket.

When they arrived, the Omnidroid was completely out of control, destroying everything in sight. Syndrome tried to use a remote control to stop it, but it even knocked *him* out.

It was up to the Supers to save the day. Individually, they were awesome, but as a team, they were unstoppable! Their old friend, Frozone, showed up and together they defeated the Omnidroid. The people of the city cheered, glad that the Supers had returned.

When the Incredibles got home, Syndrome was there. He'd just taken Jack-Jack and was flying above their house. All of a sudden, the baby turned himself into a mini-monster. The villain dropped him in shock. But Jack-Jack wasn't done yet. He ripped a valve off Syndrome's rocket boots. The villain plummeted to the ground—gone forever. Luckily, Jack-Jack ended up safe in his mother's arms.

The Incredibles went back to their normal lives. But they were ready to use their powers to keep the world safe again . . . as a family.

An Adventure to Remember

Carl Fredricksen had lived in the same house for years. All around him, things had changed. Houses had been torn down to make room for tall buildings. Now builder wanted to buy Carl's house and tear it down, too.

But Carl refused to sell. The house meant too much to him. It was where he and his wife, Ellie, had lived. Now that Ellie had passed away, Carl felt that the house, filled with memories, was all he had left.

When Carl learned that he was going to have to go to a retirement home, he came up with a plan.

"I'll meet you at the van in a minute," Carl told the men who had come to pick him up. "I want to say one last good-bye to this old place."

As the men walked back to their van, a giant shadow fell over them. They turned to see thousands of balloons rising into the air. The balloons had lifted the house off the ground!

"So long, boys!" Carl happily yelled out the window.

He was headed for the place Ellie had always wanted to go: Paradise Falls in South America.

Knock, knock, knock. Someone was at Carl's door!

Carl couldn't imagine who that could be. He was thousands of feet in the air! He opened the door and discovered a young boy named Russell. The boy was a Junior Wilderness Explorer. He had gone to Carl's house because he wanted to earn his Assisting the Elderly badge. But Russell hadn't expected Carl's house to fly away.

Inside the house, Carl and Russell were in for a wild ride. A flash of lightning cracked outside as a huge storm surrounded the house. Thunder rattled the windows, and the furniture tumbled all over the place.

Finally, the storm passed, and Carl and Russell crash-landed near Paradise Falls, South America. They both went flying off the porch.

"My house!" cried Carl as it started to float away. Grabbing hold of the garden hose, he and Russell pulled the house down . . . but not far enough to get back inside.

"We could walk your house to the falls," suggested Russell.

Making harnesses out of the garden hose, they began to pull the house.

"This is fun already, isn't it?" Russell said. "By the time we get there, you're going to feel so assisted."

Deep in the jungle, they stopped to take a break. Suddenly, Russell spotted unusual tracks in the mud. While Russell wondered what creature the footprints could belong to, he pulled out a chocolate bar and began munching on it.

Just then, a huge beak appeared from the bushes. The creature nibbled on the chocolate, too!

"Don't be afraid," said Russell. "I am a Wilderness Explorer, so I am a friend to all of nature. Want some more?" He offered the strange creature more chocolate to lure it out of the bushes.

When the creature emerged, it was the biggest, most colorful bird Russell had ever seen. He named the bird Kevin. Kevin wanted to be friends with Russell at once.

"Hey, look, Mr. Fredricksen, it likes me," said Russell. "Can we keep him?"

"No," Carl grumbled. He tried to get the bird to scram, but nothing worked. The bird followed them toward Paradise Falls.

Before long, they met another unique creature. "Hi, there," said a dog. "My name is Dug."

Carl and Russell were shocked. They'd never met a talking dog before!

"My pack sent me on a special mission," explained Dug. "Have you seen a bird?"

Just then, Kevin flew out of the bushes and tackled Dug.

"Hey, that is the bird!" Dug exclaimed. "May I take your bird as my prisoner?"

Carl agreed, but Russell said no. Dug was friendly, though. He followed them and kept asking Kevin to be his prisoner. That evening, Russell made Carl promise to protect Kevin, no matter what.

The next morning, Kevin made a noise.

"The bird is calling to her babies," explained Dug.

Russell was shocked. "Kevin's a girl?!"

Then the babies called out. Kevin set off toward her family.

Just after Kevin left, three fierce dogs appeared.

"Where is the bird?" snarled Alpha, the leader. The dogs were part of Dug's pack, but they weren't like Dug at all. They were very mean.

Alpha insisted that Carl, Russell, and Dug be brought to his master. When the dogs barked and bared their teeth, Carl realized they didn't have a choice. They had to go.

The dog pack led Carl and Russell to an enormous cave. An old man stood at the entrance, surrounded by angry-looking dogs. Carl thought the man looked familiar. "Are you *the* Charles Muntz?" he asked.

The man smiled. He was a famous explorer. Long ago, he'd found a skeleton of a bird like Kevin. But no one had believed the bird existed. Muntz had vowed not to return to America until he'd captured a similar bird.

Muntz invited Carl and Russell inside his giant airship. Carl recognized it right away. It was the famous *Spirit of Adventure.*

To Carl's delight, Muntz gave them a tour of the airship. They looked at trophies and treasures collected by Muntz over the years and viewed old photographs and artifacts.

At dinner, Muntz showed them his latest conquest. "I've spent a lifetime tracking this creature," he said, revealing a skeleton of a giant bird.

"Hey! That looks like Kevin," said Russell.

Muntz raised an eyebrow. "Kevin?"

"That's my new giant bird pet," explained Russell.

Carl knew Muntz would steal Kevin if he found him. He tried to leave, taking Russell with him.

Muntz became furious. He thought Carl and Russell were trying to steal the bird. "Get them!" he shouted to his dogs.

Outside, as Carl and Russell got the rope to the house, they heard a wail. It was Kevin! The bird scooped Russell and Carl onto her back and raced toward the cave opening, the house floating behind them.

Dug tried to stop the other dogs. But it was no use.

Muntz chased after them and even set Carl's house on fire! Carl was able to put out the flames. Meanwhile, Muntz captured Kevin and dragged the bird away.

Carl hauled his house the final steps to Paradise Falls. Russell did not help him. The boy was upset that Carl had let Muntz take Kevin and wasn't doing anything to get her back. Russell decided to try to rescue Kevin by himself.

When Carl finally got the house to exactly the right spot, he sat in his chair and looked at his wife's old scrapbook. It showed pictures of their life together. There was a note from Ellie telling him to go have an adventure of his own. Carl realized the house was just a house. His new friends were more important.

Luckily, Dug was still around. Carl emptied his house so it would fly. Then he went to Muntz's airship and rescued Russell.

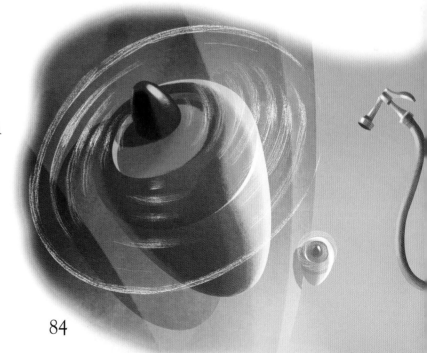

84

Kevin was being guarded by the mean dogs. Carl had an idea. He grabbed a tennis ball from his cane. "Who wants the ball?" he asked the dogs.

Carl threw the ball and the dogs chased it, allowing him to set Kevin free.

Muntz made a final attempt to capture Kevin, but his foot caught on a bunch of balloons, and the explorer drifted away. Carl's house drifted away, too. But now Carl understood that the most important memories lived in your heart, not just in your house.

Kevin was reunited with her babies, and then it was time for Carl and Russell to head home. They boarded the *Spirit of Adventure* and waved good-bye to Kevin.

Back home, Carl went to the Wilderness Explorer ceremony. Carl happily pinned a soda-cap pin his wife had given him onto Russell. He called it the Ellie badge. It was just the first of many adventures for Carl, Russell, and Dug.

A Tight Squeeze

"Calling all toys, calling all toys," Woody the cowboy announced. "The coast is clear."

It was early one morning, and Andy had just left for school. Since he would be gone all day, the toys had the room to themselves. They were ready to have some fun.

"So, Woody," Rex the dinosaur said as the toys gathered in the center of the floor, "what's this game you were telling us about?"

Woody smiled. "It's called 'sardines,'" he replied. "It's like hide-and-seek, except the toy who's 'It' is the one who hides, and everyone else tries to find him or her."

Buzz Lightyear the space ranger scratched his head. "I'm not sure I understand," he said. "What do you do when you find the hider?"

"Yeah, what do you do next?" asked Slinky Dog.

"Well," said Woody, "that's the fun part. When you find the hider, you hide with them and wait for someone else to find you both. Then, the next toy to find you hides with you, too, and so on, and so on. Get it?"

Most of the toys smiled and nodded at Woody. Bo Peep giggled. "Ooh, this is going to be fun!" she cried.

But Jessie the cowgirl was still confused about one thing. "So, by the end of the game, everyone is hiding together in one spot?" she asked.

Woody nodded. "Right," he said, "except for the last toy, who is still looking for the hiders. In the next game, that toy is 'It'—the one who hides!"

Now all the toys understood the rules and were ready to play!

"So let's decide who's 'It,'" Woody suggested. "I'm thinking of a number between one and one hundred. Whoever guesses closest to that number is 'It.'"

The toys took turns guessing. Woody was thinking of forty-nine. Hamm the piggy bank guessed forty-seven. He was the closest, so he was "It."

"Okay, everybody," Woody announced. "Close your eyes and count to twenty-five while Hamm hides."

The toys covered their eyes and began to count aloud, "One . . . two . . . three . . ."

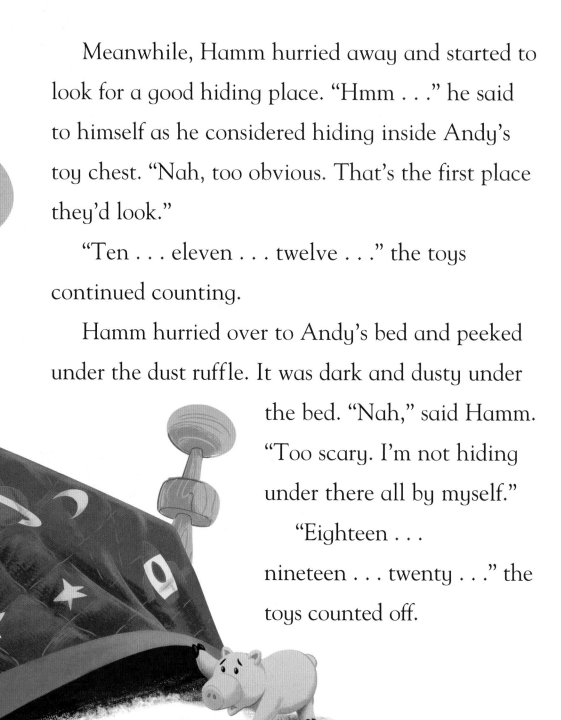

Meanwhile, Hamm hurried away and started to look for a good hiding place. "Hmm . . ." he said to himself as he considered hiding inside Andy's toy chest. "Nah, too obvious. That's the first place they'd look."

"Ten . . . eleven . . . twelve . . ." the toys continued counting.

Hamm hurried over to Andy's bed and peeked under the dust ruffle. It was dark and dusty under the bed. "Nah," said Hamm. "Too scary. I'm not hiding under there all by myself."

"Eighteen . . . nineteen . . . twenty . . ." the toys counted off.

Hamm was running out of time! With only seconds to spare, he spotted one of Andy's old lunch boxes, raced over to it, hopped inside, and closed the lid.

"Whew!" he whispered to himself. "That was close, but I'm hidden!" Only then did Hamm realize that it was even darker inside the closed lunch box than it was under Andy's bed. "Huh," he said, feeling slightly panicked but trying to keep his cool. "I, uh, wonder how long it'll take for someone to find me."

The next toy to open the lunch-box lid was Woody, whose eyes lit up when he saw Hamm inside. He glanced over his shoulder to make sure he wasn't being watched before he hopped inside the lunch box.

Soon, the lid opened and Jessie peeked in. "Yippee!" she cried. "Found ya, didn't I?"

But there wasn't much space left, so she got wedged between Hamm and Woody.

"Well, gosh, boys," said Jessie. "It's a little bit crowded in here, isn't it?"

A minute later, the lunch-box lid was lifted open, and a Green Army Man peeked in. Upon spotting the toys, he waved to his battalion. "Target located. Move, move, move!" he ordered. The Green Army Men scaled the outside of the lunch box and rappelled down the inside.

Within seconds, they were all in, and the lid was closed again.

Woody started to feel a little cramped. "Uh, Hamm," he said, "could you scooch over a little?"

"Gee, Woody," Hamm replied, "I'd like to help you out, but I'm already squished up against the sergeant here." He pointed to the Green Army Man on the other side of him.

"Hmm . . ." said Woody. "This may become a problem."

The situation got worse as more and more toys found the hiders. Slinky Dog only managed to fit inside by standing over a Green Army Man.

"Ow, your paw is in my ear," the Green Army Man told Slinky Dog.

"Sorry, there's nowhere else for me to put it," Slinky Dog said.

Buzz heard the toys complaining and located the hiding place. "Make way, folks!" he exclaimed as he piled in. But as hard as he tried, he couldn't get the lid to close.

By the time Rex found the hiders, the lunch box was completely full.

"Hey, no fair!" Rex exclaimed. "I found you guys, but there's no room for me to hide with you. What do I do now, Woody?"

"Shhhh!" Woody said, raising a finger to his lips. "Keep your voice down or everyone will come over and see where we're hiding."

But it was too late. The rest of the toys were already hurrying toward the overstuffed lunch box.

"Oh, well," said Woody with a laugh. "They've found us, so this game is over. Everybody out!"

One by one, the toys tumbled out of the lunch box and gathered around Hamm.

"Gosh, Hamm, couldn't you have picked a bigger hiding place?" Rex asked.

Hamm replied, "Well, yeah, but isn't the point of the game to get squished? Like sardines in a can? The game is called 'sardines,' isn't it?"

The toys thought that over and had to agree. From then on, every time the toys played "sardines," the hider made sure to pick a small hiding place—just to keep things interesting!

MONSTERS, INC.

Bedtime for Billy

Mike the one-eyed monster, and his best friend, Sulley, were excited about their evening. They were monster-sitting for Mike's nephew, Billy.

"Now, you be good," Billy's mother told her son.

"Don't worry, Mom, I will," he replied.

"Everything will be fine, Sis," said Mike proudly. "Sulley and I will take good care of the little guy. You don't have to worry about a thing."

"That's right," Sulley agreed.

Billy's parents kissed him good-bye and hopped in the car. His mom turned around and waved as they drove away.

The three monsters went inside and got some snacks ready. Then they ate pizza and popcorn while they watched classic movies like *Night of the Living Kids* and *Gross Encounters of the Kid Kind.*

After the movies were over, Mike and Sulley played Monster Boxing with Billy. Later, the three monsters listened to music, sang, and danced. Billy and Mike even had a video-game contest!

The night flew by, and soon it was bedtime.

"It's time for some shut-eye, Buddy," said Mike with a yawn. "Let's get you to bed!"

But putting Billy to bed wasn't going to be that easy. There was one very important detail that Billy's mother had forgotten to tell her monster-sitters.

Billy was scared of the dark!

"*Aaaaaaahhhhh!!!!*" screamed Billy.

"Wh-wh-what is it?" shouted Mike as he and Sulley ran back into the bedroom.

"There's a kid hiding in the c-closet . . ." stammered Billy. "It wants to g-get me!"

Mike and Sulley searched for human kids. They checked the whole room—once with the lights on and twice with the lights off.

"There aren't any kids in the closet," said Mike.

"All clear under the bed," announced Sulley.

"See, there's nothing to worry about," Mike said. "You can go to sleep now."

Billy was still frightened. Mike and Sulley quickly realized they had to come up with another plan to help him get over his fear.

They thought and thought. How could they show Billy that kids weren't scary?

"I've got it!" exclaimed Mike. "The scrapbook!"

"You're a genius, Mikey!" declared Sulley.

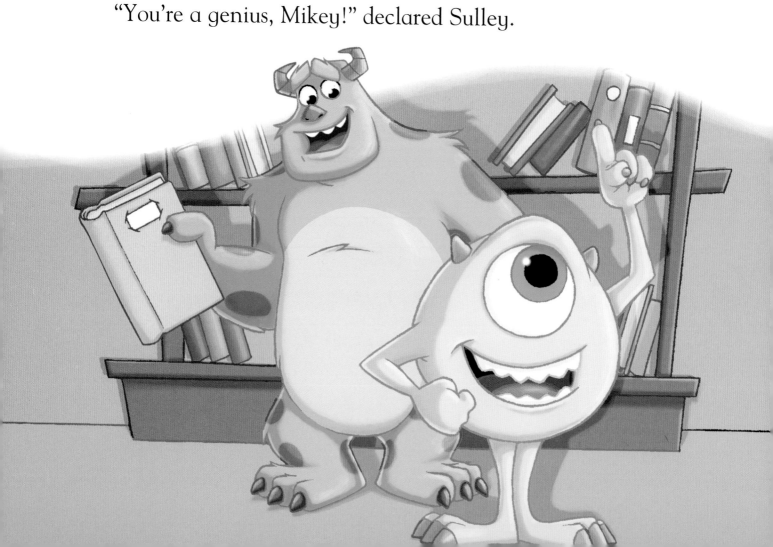

Sulley and Mike hopped onto the bed next to Billy, and the three monsters looked through the scrapbook. It was filled with snapshots of monsters with kids, newspaper clippings of them together, and laugh reports.

"See, Billy," said Mike. "Human kids are not dangerous, and they love to have fun just like you."

"And they help us!" added Sulley. "Their laughter powers our city!"

"You know, Billy, sometimes human kids get scared of *us*," said Mike. "But once they see that we're funny and friendly, they realize there's no reason to be scared of monsters."

"This scrapbook shows that there's no reason to be afraid of human kids," added Sulley. "But just in case you get scared again, you can look through it to make yourself feel better."

Billy fell fast asleep as Mike and Sulley watched from the doorway.

"Another job well done, Mike," said Sulley.

"We're still the best team in the biz," replied Mike.

Nemo and the Tank Gang

One day, a little clown fish named Nemo got into big trouble. When his father, Marlin, wasn't looking, he swam out into the open ocean on a dare. Marlin realized what Nemo had done and yelled at him to come back. Suddenly, a scuba diver grabbed Nemo and put him in a bag. "Dad? Daddy?" Nemo called, hoping his father could save him. But another diver swam up and took a picture of Marlin. The flash blinded him for a minute. The divers quickly took Nemo back to their boat and left.

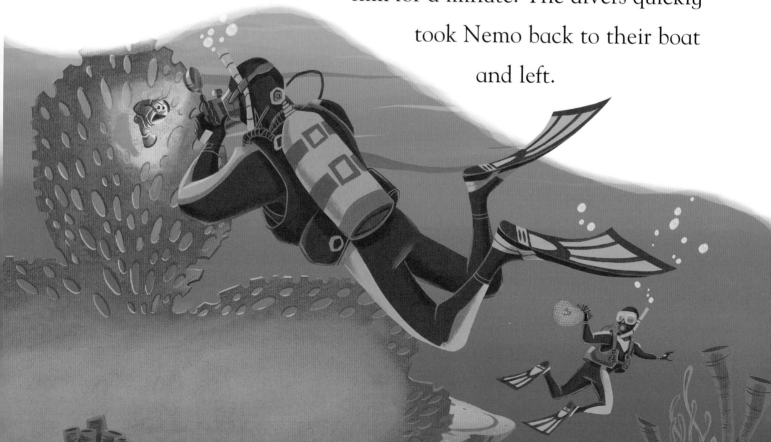

The next thing
Nemo knew, he was
being plunged into
some strange water.

The clown fish swam straight into some scary-looking Tiki
heads. He screamed and then—*bam!*—he hit a glass wall.

Nemo realized that he was in a fish tank, which was
nothing like the ocean. It had glass walls all around and was
located in a dentist's office in Sydney, Australia. Nemo had
never been so far away from home—or his father.

When the dentist peered in at him, Nemo was so startled
he bumped into a fake treasure chest, which popped open and
let out a stream of bubbles. A yellow tang fish swam over and
tried to push all the bubbles back inside the chest.

Nemo didn't know what to think. Fish didn't act like this
in the ocean.

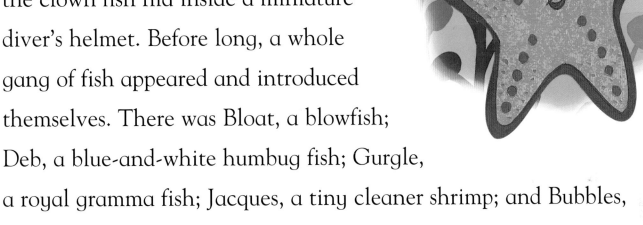

Then, a starfish named Peach
unstuck herself from the glass and
waved hello. Still a little scared,
the clown fish hid inside a miniature
diver's helmet. Before long, a whole
gang of fish appeared and introduced
themselves. There was Bloat, a blowfish;
Deb, a blue-and-white humbug fish; Gurgle,
a royal gramma fish; Jacques, a tiny cleaner shrimp; and Bubbles,
a yellow tang fish who was crazy about bubbles.

Nemo thought the fish seemed friendly. When they learned he
was from the ocean, or the Big Blue as they liked to call it, they
were amazed. Most of them had come from pet stores.

Soon, a pelican named Nigel came by. Gurgle introduced the
pelican to Nemo and told him how the clown fish had been taken
from the reef.

113

When the dentist spotted Nigel, he shooed the pelican out the open window, knocking over a frame with a photo of a little girl in it. "This here's Darla," the dentist told his patient. "She's my niece—going to be eight this week." Then he looked over at Nemo. "She's going to be here Friday to pick you up."

"She's a fish killer," muttered Peach.

Nemo panicked. He wanted to get back to his dad. He darted around the tank, but got stuck in the intake tube. "Daddy! Help me!" he cried.

A Moorish idol fish named Gill appeared from behind a plastic skull. "You can get yourself out," he said. "Just concentrate."

Nemo explained that one of his fins was smaller than the other. He didn't think he could do it. Gill showed him his own severed fin and said, "Never stopped me." So, Nemo swam as hard as he could. Before long, he had freed himself!

114

That night, Jacques woke up Nemo and led him to the volcano in the center of the tank. As they got closer, Nemo spotted the rest of the fish. He wondered what was going on.

"We want you in our club, kid," Peach explained.

"*If* you are able to swim through the Ring of Fire!" Bloat added dramatically. A wall of bubbles erupted from the volcano. The Tank Gang chanted Nemo's name, urging him on.

The little clown fish concentrated and quickly zoomed through the bubbles.

Gill smiled at him. "From this moment on, you will now be known as *Shark Bait*," he said.

"Shark Bait's one of us now," Gill continued. He paused. "Darla's coming in five days. So what are we gonna do?"

No one said anything.

Luckily, Gill had an escape plan. Nemo was the only one small enough to swim into the filter and jam it with a pebble. If he completed that dangerous task, the tank would get dirty. The dentist would have to put the fish in bags while he cleaned it. Once he did, the Tank Gang would roll their bags down the counter, out the window, off the awning, across the street, and into the freedom of the harbor.

"Let's do it," Nemo said. He was anxious to see his dad.

The next day, while the Tank Gang was waiting for the dentist to take a break, Gill told Nemo that he'd injured his fin trying to jump in the toilet during his first escape attempt.

"The toilet?" Nemo asked.

"All drains lead to the ocean, kid," Gill replied.

When the dentist left, Nemo gathered his courage, swam hard into the filter, and jammed it with a pebble. The filter blades stopped for a moment, but then the pebble slipped, and

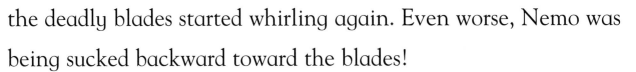

the deadly blades started whirling again. Even worse, Nemo was being sucked backward toward the blades!

His quick-thinking friends rushed into action. They pushed a plant into the tube and pulled Nemo back to safety. Gill's escape plan was ruined. The Tank Gang was silent. The Moorish idol fish swam away, ashamed that he'd put the little clown fish's life in danger.

Not long after that, Nigel heard an interesting bit of gossip. It was about a clown fish who was looking for his son. The tiny fish had battled three sharks, escaped from a hungry anglerfish, and even survived a school of jellyfish. Now he was traveling toward Sydney! A bunch of sea turtles had given him a ride, then told other ocean creatures about the clown fish's adventures. When Nigel heard the story, he was sure that the fish had to be Nemo's father. He flew to the dentist's office to tell Nemo.

At first, the little clown fish didn't believe Nigel's story. His father was too scared to swim in the open ocean. Traveling this far meant Marlin was being very brave. Now Nemo felt brave, too. He was determined to escape from the tank and find his father as quickly as possible.

In a flash, Nemo picked up a new pebble and jammed it into the filter. This time, the plan worked—soon the tank would get very dirty.

The next day, the tank was covered with green algae. Nemo knew there was a chance he might get to go home soon.

"Look at that," Gill said to Nemo. "Absolutely filthy. And it's all thanks to you, kid."

Nemo giggled. Then Gill caught Jacques cleaning and had to tell him to stop. Bloat, on the other hand, loved wallowing around in the muck.

When the dentist came in, he ran his finger along the inside of the tank. He sighed and told his receptionist he'd have to clean it before Darla arrived to pick up her new fish the next morning.

"Yay! He's going to clean the tank!" Nemo cried.

"Are you ready to see your dad, kid?" Gill asked.

"Uh-huh," Nemo said longingly.

But when the fish woke up the next morning, the tank was spotless. The dentist had installed a new filter during the night. The Tank Gang's escape plan had failed again. And Darla was due any minute!

The dentist soon arrived and scooped Nemo into a net. The little clown fish panicked, and the Tank Gang reacted quickly. They scrambled into the net with him and swam downward, forcing the dentist to drop them. The fish began to cheer, but the dentist snuck up behind Nemo and caught him in a plastic bag. Then he set the bag on the counter.

Gill and the others coached Nemo to roll the bag toward the window. He had almost made it there when the dentist noticed and moved him.

Just then, Darla came in. She was anxious to see her birthday surprise. Nemo knew he would have to do something if he wanted to survive. So he floated belly up. The dentist looked at the little clown fish and thought he had died.

Nemo winked at the Tank Gang, sure the dentist was going to flush him down the toilet. Thanks to Gill, he knew the drain would take him to the ocean.

All of a sudden, Nigel flew in with Marlin and Dory, a fish who'd been helping with the search. Marlin saw Nemo and thought he was dead. Nigel dropped the fish back into the ocean.

Darla began to shake the bag, so the Tank Gang catapulted Gill onto her head. She dropped the bag. It burst open, and Nemo landed on a tray of tools. Gill helped him get to the spit sink.

Nemo went down the drain and soon made it to the ocean, where he found his father. They were thrilled to see each other again.

Before long, the Tank Gang broke the filter and were able to find their way to the Big Blue at last!

One Amazing Chef

Deep in the French countryside lived a rat named Remy. Remy had an amazing sense of smell and taste, and dreamed of one day being a great chef. He often sneaked downstairs from the attic to secretly watch his idol, Chef Auguste Gusteau, on TV.

One day, Remy was watching TV while the old woman who lived in the house was asleep. Remy learned that Gusteau had died of a broken heart when his restaurant lost its five-star rating. He was so shocked by the news that he didn't hear the old woman wake up. She saw him and tried to catch him. Then she saw his family and friends.

"Evacuate! Move! Move!" cried Remy's father, Django. He led everyone to the riverbank to sail through a drain.

Unfortunately, Remy got separated from his family and somehow ended up in Gusteau's restaurant in Paris! It was Remy's dream come true. He watched the kitchen from a skylight.

Down below, a tall, awkward young man named Linguini handed a letter to a chef. The chef's name was Skinner. He had worked for Gusteau for many years. He was not very nice.

Linguini explained that his mother had known Gusteau. "I think she hoped it would help me get a job here," the young man explained.

Linguini was to be the garbage boy. It didn't take long for things to go wrong. He knocked over a pot of soup. Then he tried to cover up his mistake by adding water and spices to the soup.

Remy saw it all. He knew the soup would taste awful. The rat jumped down and began to add ingredients to the pot.

Linguini saw him.

Just then, Skinner entered the kitchen. "The soup! Where is the soup?" he demanded.

Linguini hid Remy under a colander. He didn't want to be seen with a rat.

Skinner saw Linguini holding the soup ladle. "How dare you cook in my kitchen!" Skinner yelled.

Before anyone could stop it, a bowl of the soup went out to the dining room. A food critic ate it, and to everyone's surprise, she loved it! Linguini knew he would have to cook again.

When Linguini and Remy were finally alone, Linguini discovered that he could talk to Remy and that the rat could understand him.

Linguini didn't want to lose his job, but he didn't know the first thing about cooking. He realized Remy could help him.

Linguini took Remy home, and they soon came up with a secret plan to cook together: Remy would sit inside Linguini's hat and tug at his hair, steering him toward the needed ingredients. They practiced with Linguini wearing a blindfold. Before long, Linguini was chopping, mixing, and cooking, just as Remy directed.

The very next day, Skinner told a chef named Colette to train Linguini. She gave him strict instructions: "Keep your station clear. Keep your arms in." She gave him tips on grating, peeling, dicing, and slicing.

"Thank you for all the advice," Linguini said.

Colette gave him a small smile. "Thank you for taking it."

Customers started to ask for more of the dishes that Linguini made with Remy's help.

Meanwhile, Skinner finally read the letter from Linguini's mother. It turned out that Auguste Gusteau was Linguini's father! That meant the restaurant belonged to Linguini. Skinner was very nervous. He had his own plans for the restaurant—and he didn't want to lose it. He knew he needed to make a plan.

Outside the restaurant, Remy ran into his brother, Emile, who led him to the rats' new home in the sewers.

Their father, Django, was surprised and pleased to have Remy back. "My son has returned!"

Remy looked around. The other rats seemed happy, but Remy knew he couldn't stay. Remy explained that he had a job with humans.

Django was upset. He explained that humans were enemies of rats.

"No, Dad," insisted Remy. He didn't think it had to be that way. He headed back to Gusteau's, determined to prove to his father that rats and humans could get along.

When Remy returned to the restaurant, he discovered the letter from Linguini's mother. He also found Gusteau's will. Remy quickly realized that Linguini actually owned Gusteau's restaurant, he just didn't know it.

Just then, Skinner arrived! Terrified, Remy grabbed both pieces of paper in his mouth and ran.

"No, no!" yelled Skinner. He chased Remy out the door and down to the river. The selfish chef couldn't let the rat escape!

Remy jumped from the riverbank onto a passing boat, using the papers in his mouth as wings. Then the rat jumped to another boat. Skinner jumped after him . . . but didn't quite make it. *Splash!* The angry little man fell into the water. Skinner floated helplessly as he watched Remy get away.

By the time Skinner returned to the restaurant, Remy had told Linguini the truth. As the new owner of Gusteau's, Linguini fired his old boss.

Over the next few weeks, the restaurant became very popular. Everyone wanted to try the new dishes Remy had been telling Linguini how to make. But Linguini was more interested in being famous than in cooking. He even held a press conference.

To everyone's surprise, Anton Ego walked into the press conference. He was the same restaurant critic who had taken away Gusteau's five-star rating. "I will return tomorrow night with high expectations," he warned.

Remy thought Linguini was enjoying all the attention a little too much. When they were alone, he pulled Linguini's hair really hard.

Linguini yelled at the rat. "I'm not your puppet!" They fought, and Remy left.

The next day, Ego arrived at the restaurant. "Tell your 'chef' Linguini that I want whatever he dares to serve me," he told a waiter.

Inside the kitchen, things were bustling. Then somebody saw Remy. He had returned!

"Rat!" someone shouted.

"Don't touch him!" insisted Linguini. "The truth is, I have no talent at all. But this rat—he's the cook."

All the cooks left, including Colette. They were disgusted.

Linguini knew he and Remy couldn't do it by themselves. He sadly went into his office.

Remy's father had watched everything from the shadows. He was surprised Linguini had stood up for the rat. "I was wrong about your friend. About you," he said to Remy.

Django whistled, and rats streamed into the kitchen, ready to help out. "We're not cooks, but we are a family. You tell us what to do, and we'll get it done."

The rats went through the dishwasher to clean themselves off. Then they were ready to cook. Remy told them exactly what to do. This time he was the chef, and Linguini acted as waiter. Colette also returned, surprised to see dozens of rats helping.

Remy made ratatouille. The delicious dish brought back wonderful memories from Ego's childhood. When Ego insisted on meeting the chef, Linguini waited until everyone had left and then brought out Remy. The next morning, Ego gave the restaurant a five-star review in the newspaper! He didn't care if Remy was a rat, only that he was a great chef.

Unfortunately, the health inspector closed down Gusteau's. But soon after, Linguini opened a new bistro called La Ratatouille. The main dining room was for humans, but a hidden dining room was reserved just for rats. Remy could be a real chef at last!

Race Day

Vroom! Vroom! Three cars zoomed around the track at the Los Angeles International Speedway. They had just started the year's biggest race: the tiebreaker for the Piston Cup championship.

The race cars were in a dead heat. There was The King, a racing legend who was looking for one more win before retirement; Chick Hicks, a tough racer who had spent his career chasing The King's tailpipe; and Lightning McQueen, the rookie sensation who had taken the racing world by storm.

Just a week ago, all three race cars had tied for first place at the Dinoco 400—a racing first. Today's tiebreaker would determine the winner once and for all.

But a lot had happened to Lightning since the Dinoco 400. In fact, he wasn't really the same race car he once had been. On the way to California, he'd had a road mishap and had ended up in Radiator Springs, a remote, sleepy town. All the cars he'd met there changed him—a lot.

At first, Lightning hated being stuck in the tiny town. He'd gotten separated from his driver, Mack, and barreled into Radiator Springs in a panic. He'd sped out of control and crashed into everything, ruining the main road.

The town had sentenced Lightning to fix the pavement before he could leave. Lightning had wanted to go to his race, but the longer he'd stayed in Radiator Springs, the more he'd gotten to know the cars who lived there. And a funny thing happened—he began to like the little town.

A rusty tow truck named Mater became his best friend. He'd taught Lightning to drive backward and to tip tractors. Sally was a blue sports car who'd taught him that the journey itself was sometimes more important than how quickly you got there. The race car had even gotten new tires from Luigi and a sleek paint job from Ramone, two other cars from town.

When the press had found Lightning, he'd been hustled into a trailer to go to the big race. He hadn't really known how to say good-bye to his new friends.

Now, the cars were fifty laps into the race. The King had a short lead, with Chick Hicks and Lightning close behind. Lightning tried to pass Chick, but Chick squeezed him out.

Lightning tried to focus on the race, but his mind drifted off. He was thinking about the wonderful drive he'd had with Sally back in Radiator Springs.

As the rookie snapped out of his daydream, he realized he was heading into the wall. He gasped and braked hard, which made him spin into the infield.

Lightning just sat there, stunned, unable to move. The other two racers were already far ahead of him. The rookie wondered if he should even keep going. The race just didn't seem as important to him anymore.

Just then, his radio crackled. "I didn't come here to see you quit," a familiar voice said. It was Doc!

Lightning looked over to his pit and saw Doc, along with a bunch of his friends from Radiator Springs: Sarge, Fillmore, Flo, Ramone, Sheriff, Guido, and Luigi. He rolled into pit row.

"Guys!" Lightning called as he entered his pit. "You're here!" The race car was so excited, he could hardly contain himself.

"It was Doc's idea," said Ramone.

Lightning looked up at the crew-chief platform. The Radiator Springs town judge and doctor, Doc Hudson, was there, wearing his Fabulous Hudson Hornet logo, just like in his glory days.

After winning three Piston Cups, Doc had gotten into a wreck. By the time he'd been fixed up, no one cared about him anymore. He'd vowed never to return to the racing circuit. At first, he hadn't taken very kindly to Lightning, but the rookie's time in Radiator Springs had taught Doc a few things, too. Now here he was, supporting Lightning.

"I knew you needed a crew chief," Doc said
to Lightning. "But I didn't know it was
this bad."

"Doc, look at you!" exclaimed Lightning. "I thought you said you'd never come back."

"I really didn't have a choice," replied Doc. "Mater didn't get to say good-bye."

Lightning looked over at the rusty, old tow truck, who grinned at him. The race car was glad to see his friend.

"All right," said Doc, getting Lightning's attention back, "if you can drive as good as you can fix a road, then you can win this race with your eyes shut. Now get back out there!"

Lightning revved his engine and sped onto the track. There was no way he was going to lose this race now!

"We are back in business!" Doc hooted over the radio.

Lightning was a lap behind. He drove hard—and began making up ground quickly. With only sixty laps to go, Lightning caught up to the leaders. Chick saw that the rookie was trying to pass him.

As Lightning tried to make a move, Chick slammed right into him.

The crash sent Lightning into a one-hundred and eighty-degree spin . . . but he kept right on going

and passed Chick while driving backward. The crowd loved it. "I taught him that!" Mater said proudly.

Lightning gave Chick a quick smile and spun back around.

Fifty laps later, it was a dead heat. Chick pushed hard and tried to overtake Lightning. Now neck and neck, they bumped into each other. Suddenly, Lightning's tires went flat.

Rubber and debris littered the raceway. Lightning headed for the pit. He had to get back out on the track before the pace car let The King and Chick go, or he'd be behind a lap. Guido changed the tires quickly, and Lightning pulled out just ahead of the pace car. He still had some ground to make up.

A few laps later, Lightning had caught up. Then the white flag dropped. This was it—the final lap. Lightning approached Chick and The King, ready to make his move.

Lightning went high around a turn. Chick tried to smash him against the wall. Lightning was sent spinning into the infield, but using a trick he had learned from Doc—turn right to go left—he recovered and took the lead, even passing The King. He was about to become the Piston Cup champion!

But Chick wasn't about to come in third. He rammed against The King. The racing veteran crashed into the wall and spun into the infield. The crowd gasped.

Lightning looked at the giant TV screen and saw what had happened to The King. He couldn't believe it. It reminded him of Doc's crash.

The rookie screeched to a stop just before crossing the finish line. He couldn't win, not like this. It just wasn't right.

Chick zoomed past him to win the race, but Lightning didn't care. He turned around and drove over to The King. The guy was a legend, and Lightning didn't want to see him end his career like this.

"What are you doing, kid?" The King asked.

"I think The King should finish his last race," Lightning answered. He drove behind the battered race car and began pushing him forward.

Everyone watched as the rookie edged The King over the finish line. The crowd went wild!

Chick celebrated his victory, but the crowd booed him off the stage. No one cared that he had won the race because Lightning had won their hearts.

Meanwhile, Lightning pushed The King over to his crew. Then the rookie headed over to his own tent, where his friends were all waiting to congratulate him. Even Tex, Dinoco's owner and the biggest sponsor of the Piston Cup, wanted to talk to him.

"Hey, Lightning," Tex said to him, "how would you like to be the new face of Dinoco?"

"But I didn't win," Lightning replied.

"There's a whole lot more to racin' than just winnin'," said Tex.

Lightning was flattered, but as he looked back at his tent, he decided to stick with Rust-eze, the small company that had sponsored him all along.

But he did ask Tex for a favor . . . .

"Woo-hoo!" Mater cried. "Look at me—I'm flying!" It was two days after the race, and the tow truck was soaring over Radiator Springs in the Dinoco helicopter. Lightning had once promised his friend a helicopter ride, and he kept his promise.

Just then, Lightning drove up to his friend Sally.

"Just passing through?" she asked.

"You haven't heard?" he answered. "Yeah, there's a rumor floating around that some hotshot Piston Cup race car is setting up his big racing headquarters here."

She smiled, and they sped away together. Lightning had found a home. He was finally happy—even though he hadn't won the big race.

To Infinity and Beyond!

One bright and sunny Saturday afternoon, Andy was playing outside. His toys were all in his room, looking for something to do.

Then Buzz Lightyear thought up the perfect activity— a launching-pad contest! He split the toys up into teams.

Each team had to design their own launching pad. The team with the most exciting launch would be the winner.

The teams worked for a little while, then Buzz got their attention. "Planning phase complete," he announced. "It's time to see which team did the best. When I say 'blast off,' you should rocket your subject across Andy's room and into the pile of pillows at the other end!"

"Let's begin with team number one," said Buzz. "Three . . . two . . . one . . . blast off!" he shouted.

Using Slinky Dog as a slingshot, Rex and Bo Peep launched Woody into the air and clear across the room.

"Yee-hah!" Woody shouted as he soared over the other toys and landed on the pile of pillows.

"Ooooooh," said one Little Green Alien, amazed.

"A mystic launch," said another Little Green Alien.

"Aaaaaah," said the third Little Green Alien.

"Team number two," said Buzz, "you're next. Three . . . two . . . one . . . blast off!"

On Buzz's signal, a unit of Green Army Men used one of Andy's T-shirts like a trampoline. They began to bounce Jessie up and down. One, two, three—each bounce was higher than the one before.

The fourth time, the Green Army Men tilted the shirt and bounced Jessie right across the room.

"Yeeeee-haaaah!" she yelled out as she was launched into the air.

"Ooooooh," said one Little Green Alien.

"Unearthly distance," said another Little Green Alien.

"Aaaaaah," said the third Little Green Alien.

"Team number three, are you ready?" Buzz asked. They nodded. "Three . . . two . . . one . . . blast off!" Buzz shouted.

And with that, Hamm and Bullseye jumped off Andy's dresser and down onto the launching pad.

Their weight shot Robot up into the air and across the room, toward the pillows.

"Ooooooh," said one Little Green Alien.

"A rocket of power," said another Little Green Alien.

"Aaaaaah," said the third Little Green Alien.

"Okay, my turn!" exclaimed Buzz. He got on RC Car. "Three . . . two . . . one . . . blast off!" Buzz rolled down the bedspread and sped onto a nearby race-car track.

At the end, the track turned upward, launching Buzz and the car high into the air.

"To infinity and beyond!" Buzz shouted as he aimed for the pile of pillows.

"Ooooooh," said one Little Green Alien.

"Cosmic momentum," said another Little Green Alien.

But the third Little Green Alien didn't say anything. He was nowhere to be found.

Just then—*squeak, squeak, squeak*—a little noise came from inside a jack-in-the-box.

Working together, two Little Green Aliens turned the toy onto one side and opened the lid. When they did, the spring within it was released and . . .

"Aaaaaah!" said the third Little Green Alien, as he took flight and soared toward the pillows. The toys all cheered. The Little Green Aliens were the winners! What a fun afternoon it had been.

A Berry Brave Troop

Princess Dot's Blueberry troop was having its weekly meeting. They were trying to figure out what to do. An ant named Teeny suggested another bake sale.

Dot was not excited about the idea. "That would be the third one this month," she complained.

Just then, Dot's friend Flik stopped by. He was a grown-up, but he and the little princess got along famously. "Hi, Flik!" Dot cried. "What's something fun we can do?"

"If you want excitement," Flik said, "just start with a new idea!"

"I know! What if we go camping at Clover Hill?" she suggested.

"That's a great idea!" cried the others.

172

But they needed the Queen's permission.

The Queen thought the Blueberries were too young to go camping by themselves.

"We'll bring Aphie," Dot suggested, pointing to her mother's pet.

"I'm afraid that's not enough," the Queen told her daughter.

"I'll go with them!" Flik volunteered.

The Queen hesitated. Flik's big ideas sometimes got him into trouble. Still, she knew the trip was important to the Blueberries, so she finally agreed.

The Blueberries cheered. They couldn't wait to go!

Dot and the rest of the Blueberries met Flik the very next morning. They were ready to begin their journey.

"Look, everyone," said Flik. "I've created a raft to get us to Clover Hill."

The Blueberries put on life preservers and eagerly got into the raft. Flik pushed off, and soon they were on their way. The raft gently bobbed down the river. After a while, Dot saw rapids ahead. "How do we steer this thing?" she asked Flik.

"Steer?" said Flik. "Well, I'm glad you asked!"

He picked up a twig and put one end in the water. Then he began to move the boat with it.

"Wow, Flik! You think of everything!" said Dot, smiling.

As they headed toward a big rock, Flik skillfully navigated them around it. "Yeah!" the Bluberries cried happily. Before long, they'd arrived at Clover Hill.

As soon as they got to shore, the Blueberry troop found a safe place to camp. Then they started to look around for food. When they had gathered some fruit and seeds, Flik called everyone over. He examined the food they had found.

"Not everything in nature is good for you—like those berries you're about to eat, Teeny," Flik said. "They are spicy and hot, hot, hot!"

"Oops!" cried Teeny. "Thanks, Flik. I don't like spicy foods."

Luckily, Dot had found some raspberries and Flik had found some sunflower seeds. They sat down and began to eat. "This is fun," Dot said. "I'm glad we came."

Suddenly, Aphie started to make a lot of noise.

"What's wrong, Aphie?" the princess asked. She whistled, and he came running. The other Blueberries looked around, but they didn't see anything unusual.

"I'm sure it's nothing," said Dot. "He probably just misses my mom."

"Let's go look for more raspberries," Teeny suggested.

"Okay," said Flik, "but first we should hide our stuff. We can leave Aphie behind to guard it."

When the ants had hidden everything, Dot gave Aphie a hug. "We'll be back soon," she told him.

The Blueberries didn't know it, but at that very moment, the grasshoppers were approaching! That's what Aphie had been trying to tell them. The grasshoppers were scary creatures. Hopper, his brother Molt, and their friend Thumper were flying low over the forest in search of food.

"Hey!" cried Molt. "I see a good place to land!"

He led the others to the exact spot the Blueberries had chosen as their campsite!

"Hey, look what I found!" called Molt just after they landed. He held up Aphie.

"I'm not interested in a little aphid!" snapped Hopper. "Go find me something to eat while I take a nap!"

But Molt thought the aphid was cute. He quickly trapped Aphie under a nutshell. Then he and Thumper set off to search for food for Hopper.

Near the berry patch, Flik looked up at the sun. "It's getting late," he said. "We should head back."

But just before they reached their campsite, Flik and the Blueberries stopped short. There were tracks in the dirt. "Grasshoppers!" Flik exclaimed.

"Grasshoppers!" The Blueberries gasped. They were scared. The grasshoppers had been nothing but trouble for the ants.

"Who knows how many there are!" cried a frightened Teeny.

"Maybe we should go home," Flik suggested.

As the Blueberries were about to head back to the ant colony, Dot stopped them.

"Hey!" she cried. "What about Aphie?"

Flik crawled over to some bushes and peeked at their campsite. Hopper was napping in the very spot where Dot had left Aphie! It was too dangerous to go get him.

But then Flik saw a nutshell hopping across the ground.
Aphie must be underneath the shell, he thought.

Flik reported back to the troop.

"How can we save Aphie?" asked Dot.

"Well, we've got something the grasshoppers don't," Flik said.
"We have big ideas." Then he gathered the girls together to
make a plan.

A little while later, Molt and Thumper returned to the campsite with some food for themselves and Hopper. After eating, Molt went to play with his new pet.

But when Molt lifted the nutshell, Aphie heard a noise. It was Dot's whistle. The grasshopper didn't know what it was, but Aphie did! The aphid ran away from Molt as fast as his little legs could carry him. He headed right up a small ridge. Sure enough, the ants were waiting for him at the top.

As soon as Aphie was safe, Flik and the Blueberries started to roll rocks down the hill. The rocks slammed into more rocks. Before long, dozens of them were headed right at Molt! The rocks hit him one after another—*bam! bam! bam!*—and knocked him over. "Whoa!" he cried.

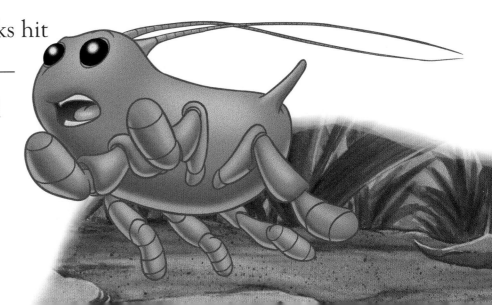

Molt slowly pulled himself out from under the rocks. Hmmm, he thought, I wonder how that happened.

But soon Molt saw a sign that said: FREE BERRIES—REALLY TASTY! He scooped up a bunch and brought them to his brother. The grasshoppers bit right into them.

"*Aaaaahh!*" they all screamed. The berries were the superhot ones Flik had warned the girls about!

The grasshoppers ran to the river and plunged their heads in, slurping the cool water.

While the grasshoppers were trying to cool off, Flik, the Blueberries, and Aphie decided to sneak out of their hiding place. They headed back to Ant Island as fast as they could!

Back at home, Dot and the Blueberries told the Queen about their adventure. The Queen was shocked when she heard they'd rolled the rocks on Molt and fooled the grasshoppers with the hot berries.

"You should have seen them dive for the water, Mom!" Dot said with a giggle.

The Queen was relieved that everyone was safe. She even congratulated Dot and Flik on their quick thinking.

"It just goes to show you," said Flik, "a few big ideas can go a long way!"

Disney·PIXAR
MONSTERS, INC.
Scared Silly

"**H**ey, Sulley, you're number one!" a yellow monster called.

"Go, champ!" yelled a striped monster.

"You're the best!" another monster cheered.

The big blue monster's friends and neighbors were cheering for him. He and his best pal, Mike, were on their way to work at Monsters, Inc.

My pal is the best Scarer in all of Monstropolis, Mike, the one-eyed green monster, thought proudly. It was the monsters' job to enter the human world so they could frighten children and gather screams.

Then they brought the screams back to Monsters, Inc. and converted them to energy. Sulley was a top Scarer.

Mike was a funny monster, though. He liked to make his friends laugh, so he worked on the Scare Floor, helping to get things ready for Sulley before each assignment. They were a great team.

While Sulley did his warm-up scare exercises, Mike brought out a door to a child's room. Then he put a scream canister in place and waited for the light to flash. As soon as the light signaled, Sulley ran through the door into the child's room.

"*Grrrr!*" Sulley growled as the door was closing.

"*Aaaaaah!*" Mike heard a kid scream.

"Wow, listen to that!" Mike cried. He was always amazed at how loudly kids screamed when they saw Sulley. Sometimes he wondered what it would be like to be a top Scarer.

That night, Mike talked to his girlfriend, Celia, about it.

"Oh, Schmoopsie-Poo," she said, "you couldn't scare a flea!"

But Mike was determined to show he could be scary—just like Sulley.

The next day, Mike carried a big black bag to work.

He waited until Sulley went to a child's room. Then he pulled a purple wig and two giant shoes with claws from the bag and put them on. "Boo!" he shouted when Sulley walked through the door.

"*Aaah!*" Sulley yelled. *Thud!* He tripped over Mike's shoes and bumped his head on the floor. "What did you do that for?" he asked, rubbing his head.

"Did I scare you?" Mike asked.

"No, but you sure surprised me!" Sulley replied.

"Oh." Mike was disappointed, but he wasn't going to give up.

That evening, Mike left work without Sulley. The big blue monster had to walk home alone. He wondered why his pal hadn't waited for him.

When Sulley got home, the apartment was dark.

"Mike, where are you?" he called.

"*Wooooooooo!*" a strange voice wailed. Suddenly, Mike jumped out from behind the kitchen door. He was covered in tomato sauce. Slimy spaghetti trailed off his ears and dangled from his fingers. "I'm a noodle monster!" he screeched loudly.

Sulley started to laugh. The more Mike tried to scare him, the more he laughed. Soon, he was laughing so hard, he couldn't stand up anymore.

Mike stared at his friend. He had been so sure the noodle monster would be frightening. But Sulley thought it was all a big joke. "I guess that means you weren't scared," Mike said.

Sulley was still laughing so hard that he was gasping for air. When he finally calmed down, he replied, "Scared? You are one great jokester, Mike!"

Mike stomped into his bedroom and closed the door.

Sulley stood outside. "Come on, Mike. Open up!" he called, knocking on the door.

"Go away," Mike answered back. He wouldn't come out.

Later, Sulley ate dinner and watched TV by himself. He didn't understand why Mike had gotten so angry. All he knew was that he missed spending time with him.

Before he went to bed that night, Sulley decided to apologize to Mike in the morning. He wasn't sure what he'd done, but he didn't want his best pal to be mad.

The next morning, when Sulley woke up, Mike had already left. So much for apologizing, Sulley thought. He walked to work by himself. Why was Mike acting so strangely? he wondered. He was usually such a happy-go-lucky monster. Maybe he was sick or had a fight with Celia.

Sulley went to the locker room to get ready. But he didn't feel much like doing his job. He was too worried about his friend.

When he opened his locker door, Mike jumped out. He was covered with blue and purple fur, just like Sulley. He was even wearing stilts to make himself tall. "*Grrrrr!*" Mike yelled loudly, waving his arms.

Sulley just stared at him. "Aw, Mike, what's wrong with you?" he asked. "Why are you making fun of me? I thought you were my friend."

"*Grrrr!*" Mike responded. Surely, Sulley must have been scared, the one-eyed monster thought.

Sulley's feelings were really hurt. He frowned and started to walk to the Scare Floor.

Mike clumped after him on his stilts. "Stop! Come back, Sulley!" he yelled. "Look at me! I'm scary like you!"

All the other monsters stopped what they were doing and began to follow Mike and Sulley. They wanted to see what Mike would do next.

"What a joker!" they shouted. "Mike, you're the funniest! We're going to bust our guts laughing!"

"I'm not funny, I'm scary!" Mike exclaimed. He took a huge breath. "Watch this!"

Mike roared. He waved his arms menacingly, but the other monsters just smiled at him. "*Rrrrrrr!*" he tried again. His pals chuckled. How come no one looks frightened? Mike wondered. That's the loudest, scariest sound I've ever made.

Then Mike's stilts flew out from under him. "*Eeeeeee!*" he yelled. *Thud!* Mike groaned as he hit the floor. "Ow, ow, ow, ow!"
"Ha, ha, ha!" all the monsters laughed.

Mike rolled to a stop beside Sulley's gigantic feet. He sat up with a moan and rubbed his head.

"Are you all right, buddy?" Sulley asked. "What are you trying to do?"

"I wanted to see if I could scare someone," Mike explained, "but I'm no good at it." The little green monster looked down sadly. "See! Everyone's laughing. Nobody looks frightened."

Sulley helped his pal stand up. "Look, Mike, that's what everyone likes about you. You make them laugh," he said. "Besides, you sure had *me* scared!"

"Oh, sure," Mike grumbled. "How?"

"Well, I thought you were going to quit being my best pal," Sulley answered. "And that's just about the scariest thing I could ever imagine."

Mike gently punched his friend's arm. Together they strolled down the hall. "Quit being your best pal?" Mike asked. "Aw, Sulley, don't make me laugh!"

A Day at School

Nemo the little clown fish loved everything about school. He loved his classmates, he loved his teachers, and he loved to learn.

Every morning, Nemo's dad, Marlin, took him to school. Along the way, Nemo always asked lots of questions.

"What is a whale's tongue like, Dad?" Nemo asked. But before his father could answer, Nemo had moved on to the next question.

"How many clown fish can a shark eat in one gulp?" he wondered. "Actually, why are we called clown fish?"

If his dad didn't know the answer, Nemo asked his teachers.

One morning before school, Nemo saw his best friends, Tad, Pearl, and Sheldon. They played tag and "algae in the middle" before school started.

Mr. Ray was on school-yard duty that morning. He was everyone's favorite teacher. Nemo and his friends swam over and sang a special song they had made up just for him.

"He's our favorite teacher.

Hip, hip, hooray

For the big, spotted manta.

We love Mr. Ray!"

Then it was time for school to begin. The first class of the day was music, taught by Señor Seaweed, an octopus. Nemo and his classmates were getting ready for the spring concert. Nemo played the conch shell. Sheldon played the clams. (The clams didn't like it very much!) Tad strummed along on some kelp. And Pearl played the sand-dollar tambourines.

"One, two, three," Señor Seaweed said as he moved his legs to the music.

Nemo and his classmates played the song over and over. One time Nemo blew his conch shell too late. Then Tad forgot to strum. And the clams got cranky.

Finally everyone got it right. Then it was time for the next class.

Nemo and his friends swam to science class. The lesson was "Your Ocean Home."

Mr. Ray was the teacher. He called on Nemo. "Where do you live?" he asked.

"An enemy, I mean emony, I mean . . ." said Nemo.

"Nemo lives in an anemone," said Mr. Ray. "While the rest of us would be hurt by an anenome's stings, Nemo brushes himself against one every day. That way the stings don't bother him."

The rest of the class looked at Nemo in awe.

"That's right!" Nemo said proudly. He liked science class. Mr. Ray always found a way to make it interesting.

Soon it was lunchtime!

There were a lot of lunchroom rules, like no inking in the lunch area and no throwing sand. And absolutely no eating of classmates, no matter how tasty they looked.

Nemo took out his lunch. "I'll trade you my kelp sandwich for your algae pizza," he said to Tad.

"Yum!" said Tad.

After lunch it was time for recess. Everyone had fun playing hide-and-seek, but then Sandy Plankton got into a bit of trouble. She swam into a clam!

Once Sandy was free, it was time for Nemo's next class. It turned out that there was a guest teacher that day—Dory! She was a regal blue tang fish who was one of Nemo and Marlin's good friends.

"Hi, Elmo!" she cried, waving to Nemo.

The clown fish giggled. Dory was very forgetful.

Dory taught the class how to speak whale.

"Repeat after me," she instructed. "*Eeyouurbawlla kaava. Pwonk! Pwonk! Froooomaafkaplewweyoo.*"

"What did you say?" the class asked eagerly.

"I just said hello!" Dory exclaimed.

Then it was show-and-tell time. Pearl brought in a cool piece of coral she had found. And Sheldon, the sea horse, had some big news—his dad was having babies!

"Who wants to go next?" asked Mr. Hermit.

Nemo raised his fin. "Today I have some very special visitors for you all to meet. Come right in, guys."

Anchor, Bruce, and Chum swam in. They were big sharks. The other kids were really scared because they thought the sharks might eat them. But Nemo told everyone how friendly they were.

"Pleased to meet you," said Chum. "Don't worry, kids, we don't eat fish anymore. Well, we try not to, anyway."

After a brief question-and-answer period, the sharks left. Everyone breathed a huge sigh of relief.

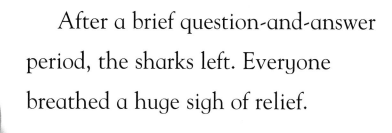

All too soon, it was time to go home. Nemo's dad came to get him. "How was your day today, son?" he asked as they swam home.

"Oh, Dad, it was awesome!" Nemo cried. "Sandy got stuck in a clam, Dory taught whale, and I brought in the sharks for show-and-tell. I can't wait till tomorrow!"

Marlin shook his head sadly. "I'm sorry, Nemo, I can't let you go to school tomorrow."

Nemo frowned. "But why?" he asked.

His dad smiled. "Tomorrow's Saturday!"

Toy Camp

"It's camp day!" Andy exclaimed as he rolled out of bed.

"Good morning, camper!" his mom called up the stairs. Andy was leaving for a week of sleepaway camp, where he would go hiking, swimming, and maybe even fishing. He was really excited.

"Finish packing your clothes and come have breakfast!" called Andy's mom.

Andy filled his suitcase with shorts, shirts, and pajamas, plus a 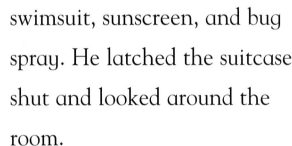 swimsuit, sunscreen, and bug spray. He latched the suitcase shut and looked around the room.

"Good-bye!" Andy said to his toys. "I'll be home soon." He picked up his suitcase and left the room.

As soon as Andy and his mother left for camp, the toys came to life. "I'm going to miss Andy," Woody the cowboy said.

"Me, too," said Hamm the piggy bank.

"Me, three," said Rex the dinosaur. "What will we do without Andy?"

"Well," said Woody, "we could play camp, too."

"That's a great idea!" Buzz Lightyear the space ranger cried.

"How do we play camp?" asked Hamm.

"That's easy," Woody replied. "We'll do everything indoors that Andy will do outdoors."

"What's the name of our camp, Woody?" Slinky Dog asked.

"How about . . . Camp Toy Chest?" said Woody.

"To Camp Toy Chest and beyond!" cried Buzz.

The Green Army Men marched out of the closet.

"I will be the camp counselor," said Sarge. He walked over to Mr. Mike. "Lights out!" he announced. "Everybody go to bed!"

"But it isn't bedtime," said Rex.

"Then let's put together tents," Sarge replied.

The toys looked around for something to use as tents.

A few minutes later, Buzz crawled out from under the bed carrying some of Andy's T-shirts. "Buzz Lightyear to Camp Toy Chest: I have found our tents!" called Buzz.

The toys helped each other pitch their tents, using pencils for poles.

"I'm too big for my tent," said Rex. As he tried to get out, he tripped over a tent pole.

So, Bo Peep found two kites and helped him make a tepee to sleep in.

"Thank you," said Rex.

"Time for bed," Sarge announced.

"It's bedtime?" Hamm asked. "Did the sun even go down?"

"No, silly," Bo Peep said. "I think Sarge is just having us practice so we're ready for the real thing. He must think this is boot camp, not fun camp."

Sarge overheard Bo Peep. Oh, *fun* camp, he thought. I can do that. "Never mind," he said. "Let's play tug-of-war instead."

The toys cheered. They tied Andy's socks together to make a rope and played three rounds of tug-of-war. During the final game, Slinky Dog stretched himself as far as he could, backing up all the way to the wall.

On the other side, Rex held onto the rope tightly, but the socks finally slipped between his claws. The toys toppled over onto each other, and Slinky Dog's team won.

Later that afternoon, Sarge ran over to Mr. Mike and announced that it was time to play Capture the Flag.

Woody explained the rules of the game to the other toys. They made flagpoles out of markers. They put a small scrap of fabric on one pole and Bo Peep's bonnet on the other to make the flags.

When they started to play, Buzz pointed at something. Rex looked the other way, and Buzz sped by him and captured the flag!

"Huddle up, team," said Hamm. "We need a plan."

"I'll scare Buzz, then Woody can run past him

and capture their flag," Rex suggested. His teammates looked doubtful. The dinosaur always tried to be scary, but he never really was. "I can do it!" Rex insisted.

So, the toys went back on the field. Rex ran over to Buzz and roared.

But Buzz didn't get scared. "Whoa, Rex," he said. "You got a frog in your throat?"

Rex frowned.

The toys played all afternoon. Everyone had lots of fun.

Soon, it started to get dark, and the toys were tired. They decided to sit around a campfire.

The toys climbed to the top of Andy's dresser and got his battery-powered night-light. They set it on the floor, turned it on, and sat around it.

"Now, let's tell scary stories!" Hamm cried.

Woody told a story about a really spooky haunted house. Everyone shivered. Next, Hamm told a story about the evil Dr. Pork Chop. At the end, Bo Peep got so frightened, she let out a little scream. Then, it was Rex's turn. He told a story about the ghost of a stegosaurus. But the toys didn't get scared. They just yawned.

"All right, now it's finally time for lights out!" called Sarge. The toys went to their tents and fell asleep.

The next day, the toys needed something to do.
"How about we go for a hike?" asked Rex.
"Sure!" cried Woody. "Counselor, lead the way!"
Sarge and the other Green Army Men led the
toys through the maze of objects under Andy's bed.
They climbed up the leg of the bed and across the

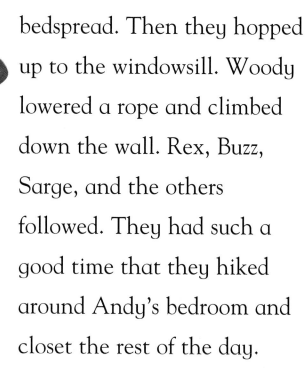

bedspread. Then they hopped
up to the windowsill. Woody
lowered a rope and climbed
down the wall. Rex, Buzz,
Sarge, and the others
followed. They had such a
good time that they hiked
around Andy's bedroom and
closet the rest of the day.

All week long, the toys had fun playing camp.

The night before Andy was to come home, the toys decided to have a talent show. Buzz was the judge.

First, Bo Peep made her sheep disappear and reappear. Then, Woody showed off his rodeo skills as he jumped on RC Car and roped Hamm. Then, the Green Army Men did acrobatics.

Rex didn't have a talent, but he had an idea. During the show, he quietly got up and hid behind a sand pail near the stage.

At the end of the show, Buzz stood up and cleared his throat. He was ready to announce the winner.

"And the winner is . . ." He paused.

Just then, Rex sprang from his hiding place and let out a mighty roar.

"*Aaaa!*" Buzz yelled. He was really frightened. He turned to run away and slipped. When he realized it was Rex who had roared, he grinned sheepishly and got up.

The other toys giggled. Rex beamed. He had finally scared someone!

Buzz turned to Rex and congratulated him. Then he gave Rex a ribbon for Best Act. The toys all clapped.

As he turned the lights off that night, Woody smiled. I hope Andy had as much fun at his camp as we did at ours, he thought.

The next morning, before Andy came home, the toys cleaned and straightened up his room. They folded his T-shirts and put them away. They put the pens and pencils back in his pencil case, and they arranged themselves neatly around the room.

Soon, Andy raced up the stairs. "Hi, everyone!" he cried. "I had so much fun at camp, but I missed all of you!"

We missed you, too, Andy, Woody thought. Welcome home.

Disney·PIXAR
MONSTERS, INC.

Mike's Dog Problem

It was business as usual at the new Monsters, Inc., where monsters collected laughs from human kids to use as energy.

Mike Wazowski was one of the top Laugh Collectors. He told funny jokes and made kids giggle a lot. But lately, he was having trouble on the job.

"Oh, no, not again!" Mike groaned as he read the paperwork for his next assignment. "This kid has a dog!"

Mike was terrified of dogs, but no one else knew. He was too embarrassed to say anything.

I can't make kids laugh when there's a dog around, thought Mike.

Those drooling fur-bags think I'm a big rubber ball!

He really didn't want to face another dog. So he needed to come up with a good excuse to skip work.

He paced the Laugh Floor, trying to think of something. "I can say I have monster pox," he said to himself.

Just then, Mike's friend, Sulley, arrived on the Laugh Floor.

The big blue monster was the new president of Monsters, Inc.

"What are you waiting for, buddy?" asked Sulley. "There are kids to crack up and laughs to collect."

"I . . . uh . . . dropped my contact lens," said Mike.

"Good one, funnyman," said Sulley as he pushed Mike toward the door. "The kids will love your new material."

Reluctantly, Mike walked through the door into the boy's bedroom. He saw the dog and immediately jumped up on a stool to get as far from it as he could. He hoped that the dog would go away so he could tell jokes in peace.

But this was a playful dog. It ran up to the stool and sat in front of Mike, who got so nervous, he couldn't remember his jokes. The boy didn't laugh at all. Mike was very upset. He would have to go back to work without any laughs.

When Mike hopped off the stool, the dog jumped up so he could shake its paw.

"*Aaaaah!*" Mike screamed and held a stool between himself and the dog. He backed toward the closet. As he was shutting the door, he noticed that the boy sitting on the bed was frowning.

Mike was sad. Kids usually loved it when he came to tell jokes. But he just couldn't relax when dogs were around.

The next day, Mike was assigned to the same room because he hadn't collected enough laughs. Sulley noticed that Mike didn't want to go. So he snuck in behind him to find out why.

Inside, Mike tried to tell a joke—but he was so nervous that he just froze with fear.

"Nice d-doggy, good d-doggy," he stuttered.

Suddenly, Sulley realized that his friend was afraid of dogs!

That day after work, Sulley asked Mike why he got scared around dogs.

"I feel like a giant chew toy when I'm near them, like any second they might bite me!" cried Mike.

"Don't worry, pal," Sulley said. "I'll show you some things to do when you're around dogs—and maybe you won't get as frightened next time you see one."

Sulley taught Mike all about dogs and gave him some safety tips. Together they read stories and watched videos about friendly dogs.

"Remember, Mike, even though dogs slobber, have big teeth, and make loud noises, that doesn't mean they're scary. We have a lot of loud, slobbering friends—just think of our pal Ricky."

Mike laughed. Maybe Sulley is right, he thought.

The next day, he and Sulley went to a room with a
dog. Mike remembered what Sulley had taught him—
to stay calm and let the dog sniff him. He took a deep
breath. The dog bounded over and sniffed Mike, who

tried to relax. He looked over at Sulley, who gave him a thumb's up. The dog was friendly, and Mike began to feel comfortable. Soon he was telling one joke after another.

Thanks to Sulley's help, Mike became the top Laugh Collector again—and he even grew to like dogs.

"Maybe *I'll* get a dog," declared Mike.

"Maybe you should start with a hamster," Sulley said with a chuckle.

Red's Tune-Up Blues

One morning, Red the fire engine woke up. The sun was shining in through the fire station door. It's the perfect day to plant a new garden, Red thought as he started his engine.

Rrrrrr. Rrrr-urr-urr. Red's engine sounded funny. *Pop! Pop! Pop!* Now loud noises were coming out of his tailpipe.

As his engine sputtered, Red tried to shrug it off. Hopefully, whatever was wrong would go away, because Red did not want to go to Doc's clinic. He'd never been, but he sure didn't like the idea of being poked and prodded. Some of the tools Doc used were awfully loud. Just the thought of going upset Red's tank.

Red decided to go for a drive. Maybe that would make him feel better.

As he drove out of town, Red passed Lightning McQueen.

"Hey, Red!" Lightning greeted him. "How's it going?"

"Fine," Red replied shyly. *Bang! Bang!*

"Whoa!" exclaimed Lightning. "That can't feel good. You okay?"

"Mmm-hmm," said Red.

Lightning watched as Red drove away. He could hear that Red's engine wasn't firing right. He's probably afraid to get it checked out, thought Lightning.

A few minutes later, Lightning got an idea. If he could get Red to race him to the clinic, maybe he could trick him into going inside.

"Hey, Red!" Lightning shouted as he caught up to the fire engine, who was turning around. The little bit that Red had already driven had made him feel worse, so he decided he would go back to town and work on the garden. Maybe that would help.

"You want to race into town?" Lightning asked him. "I'll give you a head start. What do you say?"

"Oh . . ." *Hic!* "No!" said Red, sputtering. "You're too fast."

"C'mon, Red. I'll even drive backward, just like Mater taught me," insisted Lightning. "It'll be fun."

"No, thanks," said Red. "Have to plant my flowers."

Pop! Red started driving toward town.

Lightning headed into town, too, to find his friends. They wouldn't want Red to be sick.

Lightning found everyone at Flo's V8 Café, filling up on breakfast.

"Good morning, *mi amigo*," Ramone greeted him. "Beautiful day, eh?"

"Yeah, it is," said Lightning, "except for one problem."

"What could that-a be?" asked Luigi, the tire-shop owner.

"Red's not running right," Lightning explained as he pointed to the fire engine, who was starting to plant a garden across the street. "But he's afraid to go to the clinic."

"Aw, shucks," said Mater the tow truck. "I know how the poor fella feels. I was scared my first time, too! But Doc's a pro. He'll have Red fixed up before he knows what hit him!"

"We've got to get him there first," said Lightning.

"That silly boy," said Flo. "Let me see if I can talk to him."

Flo began to drive toward Red.

Even from a distance, Flo could hear Red's engine rumbling.

"Hey there, Red!" she called out. "You're sounding a little rough this morning. When was the last time you went in for a tune-up?"

"Oh, uh . . ."

"That's what I thought," said Flo. "Honey, you need to get yourself in there."

Red looked down nervously.

"How about," continued Flo, "you go get checked out. Then, afterward, come by the café for a free tank of my best fuel?"

"Gee, Flo," said Red. "Thanks, but I'm all right." The truck went back to his flowers.

"I tell you," Flo said to her friends when she returned to the V8, "that is one stubborn fire engine."

"Don't take it personally, baby," said Ramone, Flo's husband and the owner of Ramone's House of Body Art. "Let me try."

Ramone drove over to Red. "Hey, my friend, you look like you could use some brightening up."

"Hello, Ramone," said Red. "I'm fine."

"No, really, man," Ramone said. "It's today's paint-shop special—a new coat of paint and a custom flame job, free with a visit to Doc's. You'll be the hottest fire engine around."

"Thanks, Ramone . . . but no."

Red continued with his new flower bed. Ramone could see Red wasn't making much progress. So far, he hadn't even planted one flower!

Ramone returned to Flo's. "Couldn't talk him into it," he said.

"What that boy needs is some discipline," said Sarge, who had just driven in with his neighbor, Fillmore.

Sarge rolled over behind Red. "Hut two!" roared Sarge.

"Aaaaahh!" screamed Red.

"I order you to go to Doc's in the next five minutes and get yourself a thorough once-over!" Sarge demanded.

Red just looked at Sarge and shook his head.

"Don't you eyeball me!" yelled Sarge. "Get on the street and start rolling, soldier! Move it, move it, move it!"

Red looked down and began to cry.

From across the street at Flo's everyone could see Sarge's method wasn't working.

"We had better get over there before Red drives away," Lightning said to Sally, who had just rolled up.

The two cars sped over. Mater, Luigi, Guido, Fillmore, Flo, and Ramone followed.

"Okay, Sarge!" yelled Lightning. "That's enough."

"Show him a little love, man," said Fillmore.

"Oh, well, I tried," said Sarge. He turned to Red. "I didn't mean to scare you, Red. No hard feelings, I hope."

"It's okay," Red replied, swallowing a sob. After a minute, he stopped crying.

"Oh, it is so-a nice to see two friends make up-a," said Luigi. "I tell you what, Red, since you are my friend, too, I make-a you this-a promise. You go to the clinic, I give you new set of tires. What you say?"

"Well," said Red thoughtfully, "my tires are shabby. . . ."

Everyone waited. Was Red finally going to agree to go?

"But I don't think so," the fire truck finished.

Everyone groaned. They had been so close! It looked like they would have to come up with another idea.

Then Mater thought of something. "I'll take you tractor tipping!" the tow truck promised. "Once you knock over a tractor and hear it snort, you'll be laughing so hard, you'll forget you even went to Doc's."

"Thanks, Mater, but no," said Red. "And don't worry, friends, I'll be okay." Red turned away from the other cars and looked back down at his new flower bed. He sighed. He was so tired and he hadn't gotten very far.

Bang! Pop, pop, pop! Red's engine gurgled, and more loud noises came out of his tailpipe.

"Dad gum!" said Mater. "I reckon that's about the worst sound I ever heard come out of you."

Sally decided it was time for one last try. She inched forward.

"Listen, Red," said Sally. "We all know going to get a tune-up for the first time can be scary. But whatever is wrong could be easy to fix. If you don't go now, it could turn into a bigger problem later. None of us wants you to need a complete overhaul.

We care too much about you."

Red looked back at his friends. He knew what Sally said was true.

"Will you go with me?" he asked Sally.

"Of course I will," she replied.

"We'll all go," said Lightning. "We wouldn't let you go it alone, pal."

Red smiled.

Later that day, Red rolled out of the clinic. All his friends were waiting for him.

"That wasn't so bad," he told them. "I feel great."

Doc followed Red. "He's all fixed up, guys, and healthy as a horse!" Doc proclaimed.

"All right, Red!" said Lightning. "How about that race?"

"Okay," said Red, "and then I'll plant my flowers."

"You go ahead," said Lightning. "I'll be ready when you are."

Red revved his engine. *Vroom!* It sounded smooth as silk. He took off.

As Lightning started to catch up, Red turned his siren on full blast. *Wooooo-woooooo.*

Lightning was so startled that he veered off the road into the bushes. Sally, Doc, and the other cars giggled. Red smiled and sped forward. It was good to be running on all cylinders again.

Who's In Charge?

"Now, Dory," said Marlin the clown fish, "Nemo has to do three things while you're watching him this afternoon: science homework, conch-shell music practice, and anemone cleaning. Now say that back to me."

Marlin was a little worried. His friend Dory, a regal blue tang fish, was very forgetful. Would she remember what his son, Nemo, was supposed to get done?

"He needs to . . . um . . . oh, it's right at the tip of my tongue," Dory said.

"Science homework, conch shell, clean the anemone," said Nemo. "I got it, Dad. No problem."

"That's right! What he said," Dory agreed.

Marlin sighed.

"We'll be fine, Dad," Nemo said. "Don't worry."

Finally, Marlin waved good-bye to them and swam away to do his errands.

As soon as he was gone, Dory began swimming in circles around Marlin and Nemo's anemone home. "Hee, hee, hee!" she laughed. "Nemo, betcha can't catch me! No way! 'Cause you're too slow. . . ."

Nemo sped toward her and chased her around the anemone a few times. It was fun, and Nemo wished they could play all afternoon. But he knew they couldn't. So he stopped chasing Dory and tried to get her attention.

"Dory, come on," Nemo called to her. "That was fun, but now I'd better get started on my science homework."

Dory swam over. "Your science homework?" she said as she tried to catch her breath. "Aw, can't you do that tomorrow?"

Nemo shook his head. "Like my dad said, I have to do it this afternoon," he explained. "It's due tomorrow."

Nemo explained his assignment to Dory: he had to find a sand dollar to bring to class the next day.

So the two fish swam around the reef, looking for a sand dollar. Before long, Nemo spotted one lying on the seafloor under a coral outcropping. He picked it up gently.

"I found a sand dollar!" Nemo exclaimed. "It looks really cool!"

"That's fantastic!" replied Dory. "Now we can play!"

But Nemo reminded her about their to-do list. "No, Dory," he said. "Now I need to practice my music."

264

"You do?" said Dory, sounding disappointed.

Nemo sighed. "Didn't you hear my dad say that?" he asked.

"Oh," Dory said. "That's news to me, but all right."

"I have band practice tomorrow at school," Nemo explained.

They swam back to the anemone. Nemo put his sand dollar away and got out his conch shell.

"Yeah, play it, Nico!" Dory exclaimed as she grooved to the tunes.

Nemo smiled. Sometimes Dory even forgot his name. Nemo played and played until he felt ready for the next day.

"Thanks, Dory!" he said at last. "We're done."

"Yippee!" she shouted, swimming excitedly around Nemo. "Now it's playtime!"

But Nemo remembered their work wasn't done yet. "Not quite, Dory," he said. "I have to clean the anemone first."

Together, Dory and Nemo tidied up the zooplankton crumbs that were cluttering the anemone. A few minutes later, the place was spotless.

"Thanks for helping me, Dory," said Nemo.

"You're welcome," she replied. "What do you want to do now?"

Nemo laughed. "I want to play!" he said.

"Now, that's a crazy idea," Dory said. "I like it!"

So Nemo and Dory played tag all afternoon. Dory kept forgetting who was "It." Even so, they had a lot of fun chasing each other until Marlin got home.

"Hi, Dad!" Nemo greeted him.

"Hey, Nemo!" Marlin replied. "Hi, Dory. How was your afternoon?"

"Great!" Dory cried.

"Yeah, great!" Nemo agreed. "I did my science homework, practiced my conch shell, and cleaned the anemone. And we even had time to play!"

Marlin looked impressed. "Wow," he said. Then he turned to Dory. "Good job, Dory. Thanks for watching Nemo and making sure he got everything done. I really appreciate your work."

"Aw, don't mention it," Dory replied humbly.

Nemo couldn't believe it! All afternoon, Dory had just wanted to play. Nemo was the one who had reminded *her* about what he needed to get done. And now his dad was giving Dory all the credit!

"But, Dad . . ." Nemo started to object.

Marlin looked over at Nemo and gave him a knowing wink—and Nemo understood. His dad *did* know the truth, and he was very proud of his son.

That was all the credit Nemo needed.

"Yeah, Dory," said Nemo, patting her on the back. "You're good at being in charge."

THE INCREDIBLES

A Super Summer Barbecue

One hot summer afternoon, Helen Parr stood in the kitchen frosting a chocolate cake. Her daughter, Violet, lay on the couch reading a magazine. Jack-Jack, the baby, sat in his high chair eating.

"Dash!" Helen called to her other son. "It's almost time to leave for the barbecue."

"Hey, Mom," complained Dash, running into the room at Super speed, "why do we have to go to some silly neighborhood barbecue?"

"Dashiell Robert Parr," said Helen, "we're lucky to have been invited. It's our first neighborhood party. You know we're doing our best to fit in here. And remember: *no* Super powers outside the house."

"Right, Mom. No Super powers. The barbecue should be *loads* of fun," said Dash, rolling his eyes.

Just then, Jack-Jack threw a bowl of mashed peas. In a flash, Helen stretched her arm across the kitchen and caught the bowl in midair. Helen's Super powers as Elastigirl could come in pretty handy around the house, but she knew if her family's powers were ever discovered, they would have to move again.

Bob Parr walked in through the front door. "Honey, I've got the lawn looking shipshape," he said as he flexed his muscles. Bob used to fight crime on a daily basis as the Super, Mr. Incredible, but now his biggest weekend battle was the crabgrass. He sighed. "I finally got the last of that giant tree stump. If I could have used my Super strength, I would've been done three hours ago."

"You're right, dear," Helen answered, giving him a kiss on the cheek. "But you know we have to do our best to behave like a normal family. I only have a few more boxes to unpack, and I *don't* want to move this family again."

"No one will ever believe Violet is normal," said Dash.

Violet jumped up from the couch. "You be quiet!" she shouted. Then she threw a force field in Dash's path, knocking him to the ground.

"Kids, kids! That's enough. Let's get ready to go," said Helen.

A while later, the Parrs walked around the block to their first neighborhood barbecue. Helen smiled at Jack-Jack, who was in a baby backpack. "I hope they like my cake," she said as she walked to the dessert table.

Bob headed over to the grill to help out. Violet looked around for someone to talk to.

Dash watched some kids compete in a sack race. He couldn't race because it might reveal his Super speed.

Then a boy walked up to Dash. "Are you too chicken to play? *Bawk-bawk-bawk*," clucked the boy, flapping his arms. Some of the other kids laughed.

Dash scowled. If only I could race, I'd show that kid. When the mean boy hopped by, he mysteriously tripped and fell.

"Weird," the boy said. "It felt like someone tripped me."

Dash smiled to himself and brushed off his sneaker. His speed had come in handy, after all. Luckily, his mom hadn't seen him.

Meanwhile, Helen was getting to know some other mothers and toddlers. She listened carefully as another woman talked about removing grass stains. When the woman began to discuss needlepoint, Helen realized that Jack-Jack had crawled away.

Out of the corner of her eye, Helen saw Jack-Jack atop a high brick wall. He was about to topple off!

In a flash, Helen shot her arm all the way across the yard and caught him. She sighed with relief and hugged Jack-Jack close to her. The other mother just rubbed her eyes and mumbled something about not sleeping much the night before. Oops, Helen thought to herself.

Over by the grill, the men talked about the previous night's baseball game. When the steak was ready, Bob stepped forward. "Allow me," he said, as he picked up a knife. This steak is a bit tough, he thought. I'll just cut a little harder.

Craaack! All of a sudden, the table splintered in two. The meat went flying and landed in the dirt. Guess I used a little too much Super strength, Bob thought.

"They just don't make tables like they used to, do they fellas?" Bob asked, as the others laughed politely.

277

Violet hadn't found anyone her age, so she sat under a shady tree and began to read. Then an old lady came over. Violet stood up to introduce herself. Once she did, the woman wouldn't stop talking. She told Violet about her miniature duck collection, her dentures, and even her hot-water bottle.

Finally, Violet couldn't stand it anymore. As the woman reached step thirty-three of her potato salad recipe, Violet pointed at something.

The woman turned, and Violet seized the moment. She jumped behind a tall plant and used her Super powers to make herself invisible. Even though only her body disappeared, the colors of her clothes blended in with the bushes.

Minutes went by. Finally, the lady noticed that Violet wasn't standing next to her. She looked all around and then walked away. When the coast was clear, Violet reappeared. She smiled to herself as she sat back down and opened her book.

Since the steak had fallen on the ground, Bob and the other guys decided to grill some hot dogs and hamburgers. Bob didn't help this time, but he did eat one or two more hot dogs than he should have.

Helen couldn't have been more pleased to see the neighbors enjoying her chocolate cake. Someone even asked for the recipe. She looked around the yard and spotted Dash telling a story. Violet was eating an ice cream cone with a girl her age.

Wow, it looks like we really fit in here, Helen thought as Bob walked over to her. He was finishing another hot dog.

Just then, she overheard one of the neighbors. "There's something strange about those Parrs," he said.

Helen grabbed Bob's arm. Bob looked at her. Had someone discovered them? Were their Super powers about to be revealed?

"Yeah, you should see how Bob mangled the table—and the steak!" a second neighbor said.

"Grandma said that Violet acted like she'd never heard of potato salad," a third neighbor chimed in. "And my son said Dash just *watched* the other kids race."

"All that may be true," someone else added, "but that Helen sure makes a terrific chocolate cake!" Everyone agreed, and the conversation ended.

The Parrs sighed with relief and chuckled to themselves. Their cover wasn't blown after all!

Maybe they were a little strange compared to the average family, but they were doing their best to act normal. Bob and Helen rounded up their kids and headed for home, pleased with the way things had gone.

"I think we could really like this neighborhood, Bob," said Helen, as they reached their house. Then she gave him a great big kiss, which the kids did their best to ignore.

"I think you're right," answered Bob. "I've got a good feeling about things this time."

"Sweetie, would you mind moving the car over a bit?" asked Helen. "I need to get out of the garage to go grocery shopping tomorrow morning."

"Sure thing, honey," answered Bob. "I'll be right in."

Bob looked at the car sitting in the driveway. The street was quiet. It's too easy, he thought to himself. Besides, a guy's gotta work out every now and then. Bob picked up the car, balanced it on one finger and put it down on the other side of the driveway. Dusting off his hands, he turned around to find Rusty, a little neighborhood boy, sitting on his tricycle with his mouth hanging open.

"Uh, have a good evening, Rusty," said Bob, giving him a little wave. Then he went inside and enjoyed the rest of the evening with his Super family.

A New Adventure

Over the years, Andy had a lot of fun playing with his toys, especially Buzz and Woody. He took them just about everywhere, from birthday parties to Pizza Planet.

The years passed quickly. Before the toys knew it, Andy was getting ready to go to college.

The toys were upset. "We knew this day was coming," Woody said.

Andy began to pack. He decided to take Woody to college. He put his other toys in a bag that would go in the attic.

A little while later, Andy's mom went to his room. She saw the bag and thought it was garbage. Soon the toys were out on the curb.

By the time Woody got outside, the toys had found a box in the family car that was set to go to Sunnyside Daycare. They decided to climb in. They didn't think Andy wanted them anymore.

Woody tried to explain. "He was putting you in the attic. I know it looks bad, guys, but you've got to believe me."

"Andy's moving on," Jessie said. "It's time we did the same."

Just then the doors closed and the car started moving.

The toys soon arrived at Sunnyside Daycare. There were kids everywhere. "We hit the jackpot, Bullseye," Jessie the cowgirl said.

Soon a bear named Lotso appeared. "Welcome to Sunnyside, folks!" Lotso seemed very nice. He explained that the toys would get played with everyday.

Rex the dinosaur couldn't wait for recess to end.

But Woody wasn't excited about playing with the day-care kids. "You have a kid—Andy," he reminded the others. "Now I'm going home."

The other toys wouldn't leave, though. "It's over. Andy is all grown up," Jessie said.

Everyone but Woody stayed.

Woody snuck onto the roof of the day-care center and tried to fly a kite back to Andy's. He fell into a tree, and a little girl named Bonnie found him. She took the cowboy home and introduced him to her toys.

At Sunnyside, the kids finally returned from recess. Andy had always taken good care of his toys, but these kids were very young and played roughly. Soon Slinky Dog's spring got all tangled up, Jessie's hair was used as a paintbrush, and Hamm the piggy bank was covered with glue and glitter.

The toys knew they had to do something or they would never last. Buzz went to see Lotso. He asked if the toys could go to another room, where the kids were gentler.

Lotso told Buzz that he could move, but everyone else had to stay where they were. But Buzz refused. He didn't want to leave his friends behind.

Then Lotso and his gang pushed Buzz's RESET button. Buzz didn't remember any of his friends, and he couldn't warn them that Lotso and his gang didn't care about them.

When the toys realized they wanted to go back to Andy, Lotso and his gang appeared. Buzz was with them.

Lotso didn't want the really young kids to play with him. So he made sure Andy's toys stayed right where they were by trapping them in storage baskets.

Back at Bonnie's house, her toys told Woody what had happened to Lotso. A girl had once loved him, but when he'd gotten lost, she'd replaced him and didn't need him anymore. Lotso had never forgotten, and he never liked new toys.

Woody realized his friends were in danger. He had to save them. He snuck into Sunnyside Daycare and found his old pals. "We're busting out of here tonight!" he said.

Woody and the others found Buzz. They pushed a button on him and he went into Spanish mode. But he was on their side again. "C'mon, El Buzzo," Woody said.

They snuck outside and made it to a Dumpster. But Lotso and his gang were waiting there. All of the toys fell in the Dumpster, including Lotso. Soon a garbage truck emptied it. Buzz hit his head and went back to being his old self.

Andy's toys discovered a way out. But Lotso got stuck. Buzz and Woody knew they had to save him, no matter how mean he was.

Once Lotso was free, the toys ended up on a conveyor belt. They were headed toward a fiery shredder. They yelled at Lotso to push the emergency STOP button. But he wouldn't. He left them there.

The toys were worried, but luckily the Little Green Aliens had found a crane. "The claw!" they exclaimed. They used the crane to pull the toys to safety.

The toys made it home, just before Andy left for college. They all hopped into the box that was meant for the attic. Woody wrote a note on it, telling Andy to take the box to Bonnie's house.

Andy showed Bonnie each of the toys. "I need someone really special to play with them," he said.

Buzz and Woody watched as Andy drove away. "So long, partner," Woody said. He would miss Andy, but he would always remember how much fun they'd had. And now he and the others had a great new kid who would love them.